BOISE BELLE

Spur plowed his fist into the man's chin, sending him reeling across the coach to the opposite seat. Coughing, choking on the dust that spun in through the opened window, Silas renewed his attack. McCoy's foot connected with his stomach and sent him back.

"Damn!" Silas said, rubbing his gut. "You're asking for it."

Spur drew before the gunman had even grasped the Dragoon's holster. "This ain't no place for shooting," he said in an even voice.

SPUR #30

BOISE BELLE

DIRK FLETCHER

LEISURE BOOKS NEW YORK CITY

A LEISURE BOOK®

November 2005

Published by

Dorchester Publishing Co., Inc.
200 Madison Avenue
New York, NY 10016

ISBN 0-8439-2820-4

Printed in the United States of America.

Visit us on the web at www.dorchesterpub.com.

BOISE BELLE

CHAPTER ONE

Silas Mander wouldn't take no for an answer.

"Come on! Show me your piece! Bet it won't stand up to this little baby!" The mustachioed gunman twirled his gold-plated Dragoon revolver as the stagecoach creaked along a rutted track. Dust laden sunlight shone on its walnut handle.

Sitting across from him, Spur McCoy sighed. "Don't you believe in getting the latest? The relic must date back to 1848."

"It do," the balding man said, nodding. "I just keep what's worked for me. Now you gonna show me your pea shooter or am I gonna have to—"

"Have to what?" Spur sighed. "Here." He unholstered his weapon and handed it to the man.

Silas took it and guffawed. "Hell, an old Navy revolver? This thing couldn't hit a—a—holy shit!" He stared down at it. "I'll be damned!"

"What's wrong now?" Spur tried to make more room for himself on the seat. The two men on both sides of him seemed to be taking up more than their fair share.

"What's wrong? What's wrong?" Silas thundered. "I'll tell you what's wrong! That's mine! That's my old piece! Lost it to a sonofabitch thief on the trail outside Phoenix last year. And you're him!" His nostrils flared.

"No." Spur clamped his hands on the man's.

"Nothin' doin'! That's my revolver! I oughta kill you right here and now, you thieving bastard!"

McCoy pried his revolver from the man's grip. "You're wrong, Mander. I've had this for four years. Picked it up in St. Louis. Griswold's Firearms, if I remember the name right. Have a bill of sale in my bags."

"Like hell!"

"Rein it in, Silas," the man to his right said. "You're keeping me awake!"

His face beet red, Mander made a fist. McCoy rocked left when Silas drove it into the stagecoach wall. As the wood splintered and the big man howled, Spur calmly holstered his revolver.

"You've got some kind of nerve, Silas. One revolver looks like any other," Spur said.

"Not that one!" Mander massaged his hand and sat back on the seat. "It had a snaky picture in the grain on the handle. I swear that's mine!"

"You heard him," the passenger beside Mander said.

"No!" Mander grabbed his Dragoon. "Now we'll see whose it is!" He levelled it at Spur's chest.

"Jesus! You could shoot someone with that thing!"

"Yeah, Reinhart. Him! I'll plug that thievin' bastard!"

Spur shook his head. "Use it or holster it!" he shouted.

Silas stared at Spur, sweating, his upper lip curling under his black mustache. He hesitated.

"Go ahead! Just kill me and take it!" McCoy's voice was harsh. "But remember this day when you feel the rope tighten around your scrawny neck and squeeze the breath outta you! Remember how your stupidity cost you your worthless life!"

Mander eased off on his aim. "Well, well," he stammered.

"Gentlemen," Reinhart said, brushing off his black suit. "Can we keep this civilized?"

"Well, I don't wanna hang if I'm wrong." He holstered his revolver and lunged at Spur. "We'll just see if I am!"

Spur grabbed Mander's hands and threw them off his gunbelt. "Jesus!" he cursed.

Undaunted, the big man threw his weight against Spur, falling on him, legs and arms flailing. The men on both sides of McCoy groaned as the two grappled.

"It's mine!" Mander screamed.

"No!"

They fought it out. Spur plowed his fist into the man's chin, sending him reeling across the coach to the opposite seat. Coughing, choking on the dust that spun in through the opened windows, Silas renewed his attack. McCoy's foot connected with his stomach and sent him back.

"Goddamn!" Mander said, rubbing his gut. "You're asking for it."

Spur drew before the gunman had even grasped the Dragoon's holster. "This arn't no place for shooting," he said in an even voice.

"Damn right."

"Shut up, Reinhart!"

Three explosions broke through the relentless clatter of the stagecoach and the horses' pounding hooves.

"Jesus, what was that?" Silas asked.

Spur looked out the window. "We got company, men."

"Indians?" Mander looked at him.

"No. White men." He ducked back inside. "Three of them. Kerchiefs around their faces. And they're shooting." He stared at Silas Mander. "Friends of yours?"

"They're still pretty far back," Reinhart said, peering through the window. "Out of range."

The men drew their weapons.

"Now's a good time to show me what you can do with that thing, Mander!" Spur shouted, and peeled off a warning shot toward the advancing gunmen. It was quickly returned.

"Hell!"

"What's the matter, Silas? Ain't up to a little gunplay?"

"No, it's not that, it's just . . . ."

"Save it for later!"

The driver rode the horses as hard as he could, forcing them to a gallop as they tugged the heavy load. The stagecoach bounced and bucked like a wild steer. Spur tried to steady his legs as he took another shot.

"Funny that they ain't gettin' any closer," Feingold said.

"Yeah. This stage isn't moving that fast." Spur craned his neck. The three mounted gunmen seemed to be riding just out of range.

"What in hell's going on, Geoffrey?" Silas said to the thin man seated beside him.

"Damned if I know!"

"Maybe they're driving us into a trap." Spur glanced out again. "But there doesn't seem to be a good place for an ambush up ahead."

Mander fired two shots.

"You're wasting lead, Silas!" Geoffrey said.

"I know, but I gotta do something!"

Spur thought hard. "There's nothing we can do, men. Nothing except wait this out and see what happens." He settled back on the seat. "This happen much around these parts?" McCoy asked the fellow on his right.

"Nope. It don't happen nowhere. Something mighty strange going on here."

"Yeah. Are they still hanging back, Reinhart?" Spur asked.

"Yup. No way we can hit 'em from here."

"And I don't suppose the driver'll slow down none to let us shoot 'em."

"I don't understand!" Silas said.

Three more shots boomed out behind the rollicking stagecoach.

"Boise's gonna be the most glorious sight a man could see," Reinhart said.

"Yeah."

The gunmen took a few more shots. Then silence.

"Well, that's it, men," Spur said as he looked out the window. Yellow dust boiled up in the air around the retreating horses. "They're heading back."

Silas Mander smiled smugly. "We scared 'em off."

Reinhart shook his head. "Hell, Mander. You got crazy ideas. We didn't scare them off."

McCoy grinned. "Obviously not. It's almost as if they didn't want to hit us. Didn't even want to stop the stage."

"Maybe they decided we didn't have anything worthwhile." Reinhart scratched his chin and took one last look out the window. "Maybe they had second thoughts."

"No, that's not it at all. I know exactly what those men were doing—what they were hired to do."

Spur turned to the thin man seated beside him. "How?"

He smiled. "I'm Geoffrey Evans. My father's the governor of Idaho Territory."

"So? That make you an expert on thieves?" Silas said.

Geoffrey ignored him. "My father sent me a letter telling me the trouble he's been having. It's almost election time and someone's trying to scare him off. They stole one of his horses, knocked down the front door of the governor's mansion, sent him threatening letters—and now this. Seems likely they knew I was on the stage and decided

I was as good as my father to harass."

Spur nodded. "I've heard about your father, and what's been happening in Boise."

Geoffrey smoothed out his corduroy pants legs on his thighs. "Just another indirect attack on the Territorial governor, as far as I can tell."

"I see," McCoy said.

He knew all about Martin Evans. In fact, the Secret Service was sending him to Boise to look into the man's complaints that someone, or a group of men, were out to kill him.

"Is your father really fearful of his life? Does he believe someone'll kill him?"

"Maybe. That's why I'm going home for the day. I'll be heading back in the morning." Geoffrey Evans smiled. "My father wants some free legal advice."

"Well, lawyer," Spur said. "What do you think of Silas there?" He glanced at the man. "Should I charge him with attempted murder?"

"Now hold on, stranger!" Mander sighed and straightened his shoulders. "Push yer piece out here. I won't touch it, I'll only look at the handle."

Grinning, Spur held it between the seats. Silas peered at the walnut grain and finally sat back.

He coughed. "Guess I was mistaken. Ain't no snake on that handle."

"Only snake around here's you, Mander!" Reinhart said.

"Well hell! You can't blame a man for looking out for himself," Mander said.

"Sure, when he's got his eyes closed." Spur pushed the revolver into his holster. Boise wasn't far now. Boise and Governor Evans.

"It only makes sense. Those men were attacking my father through me." Geoffrey shook his head. "Sometimes I wish he'd never gone into politicking."

"He might think the same thing." Spur kept an eye out for the gunman until they'd safely pulled into Boise, Idaho.

CHAPTER TWO

"So what do you think about my father's town?" Geoffrey Evans asked him as the stagecoach rattled into the bustling heart of Idaho Territory.

"I won't know until I see it." Spur looked out the window as the driver reined in the horses. "Looks like a fine enough town. But looks don't tell a man everything."

"I know what you mean."

As his boots dug into the inch-thick dust of Goldrush Street, Spur wiped trail grit from his face and thought about his assignment. His superior's telegram had been concise. General Halleck wanted Spur to halt the terror that had been stalking Governor Martin Evans for the past few weeks as election day grew nearer.

McCoy slipped his hat off his forehead and ran a bony hand through his hair, waiting for his carpetbags to be thrown down from atop the stage. If it stayed as hot as this, he thought, he wouldn't even want to touch a woman even if he did find one—and she was willing.

Though it probably got cooler after dark.

"What's the holdup?" Spur finally yelled to the driver, who stood on the seat and rummaged through the bags.

The grizzled man winced. "My shoulder's what it is! Darn thing's acting up again." The driver stepped aside. "Git 'em yourself!"

"Alright, alright." McCoy sprang up and reached for his bags. "Hard to get good help these days," he muttered.

"And that brown leather one!" someone said below him.

"Yeah and the green bags!"

Spur dropped the dirty luggage into the street, finally found his at the back and hauled them down.

"Mighty nice of you, McCoy," Geoffrey Evans said, gripping his oversized, heavy leather bag.

"No problem," he huffed. "Is your father expecting you? Think he'll be home in an hour or so?"

The lean man smiled. "Possibly. My father isn't one to keep schedules. Poor mother, before her untimely death, had to put up with him working all night. Burned more midnight oil than counterfeiters—if you know what I mean."

Spur nodded. "I'll track him down. Where's the governor's place?"

"You'll find the mansion, as my father likes to term it, at the end of Thistledown Avenue. It's a big brick thing. Take one look at it and you'd swear you were back east." Geoffrey laughed.

"Fine. Thanks." McCoy trotted across the street to the Goldrush Hotel and got a room.

A half hour later, wearing clean pants and a slightly wrinkled blue shirt, Spur found the street. Two blocks of Thistledown extended from either side of Goldrush. Governor Evans' place was the showpiece of Boise. The two story brick monstrosity, surrounded by a six-foot iron fence, dominated one end of the short street. Smoke rose from one of the spiralled chimneys.

He moved toward it, tipping his hat and greeting a few residents. Boise was a fairly large town. He certainly hoped the governor had some leads.

McCoy found the gate open and looked up at the brass eagle that surmounted it. His boots clicked on the brick walkway that led to the front porch. Manicured gardens extended down both sides of the big house—he hadn't seen roses for years. Their scent hung in the air, reminiscent of a certain blonde-haired woman lost in his memories of St. Louis.

The doorknocker banged twice on the solid oak door. Spur waited until it whipped open.

"Yes?"

He instantly took off his hat. "Ma'am, I'm looking for Governor Evans."

The petite girl smirked. "So am I." She shook her head. Soft, curled blonde hair spread out like a halo around her. "My father's been gone all day long, and Geoffrey's waiting to see him. Honestly, you'd think he'd have time to talk to my brother." The thin-nosed girl smiled sweetly. "I'm terribly sorry, he isn't here. Who may I say called?"

"McCoy. Spur McCoy."

She glanced down at his boots. "You, ah, aren't wearing any, Spur. I mean—Mr. McCoy." Her gaze slowly trailed back up to his face.

"Just when I need them, ma'am. Tell your father I'm staying at the Goldrush Hotel. I'll stop by to see him again in the morning."

"Okay. If you have to go . . . ."

He grinned, planted his low-brimmed Stetson on his head and turned.

"Do come back in the morning," the girl called out. "I'm sure he'll be here!"

"Fine. I'll do that."

She couldn't hide the urgency in her voice, McCoy thought as he walked out through the gates and onto Thistledown. How old was she? Sixteen? Seventeen?

Probably too young. He stifled a yawn as he returned to the Goldrush Hotel. Maybe he should rest up for a night. A good stretch of shut-eye would feel good.

A yellow half-moon nearly touched the western horizon, scattering scant light on the countryside.

The five men gathered a half mile out of town. Mounted, kerchiefs covering their faces from the eyes down and hats pulled low over their heads, they waited. The horses whinneyed and jostled on their legs. They were eager to be off, and so were the men.

Finally, a sixth rider quietly approached from the east. The assembled men watched, straightening their backs, clearing their throats.

"You all made it. Good. We know what we have to do," the gruff-voiced rider said.

They nodded.

"Then let's go!" he shouted. "Let's do it for the town, for the people of Boise. Things have gotten out of hand. No one's in control of him. Are we gonna let that man get away with it? Are we gonna let him live?"

"Hell, no!" one called out.

"That's the spirit. Let's ride back to town and wipe that scum off the streets!"

The men fell in behind their leader at a slow trot, saving their horses.

At nine they slipped into town and, without talk, headed toward the Lucky Dollar Saloon. As they rode down Goldrush Street, other riders and men walking along its broad avenue moved aside. Eyes turned to watch them go, but no one challenged the men who wore the kerchiefs.

"Good, no trouble," their leader whispered as they gathered across the street from the green batwing doors that led into the bright saloon. Raucous laughter and the slap of the boots on the floorboards echoed from inside.

Weapons drawn, the six men waited for the right man to step outside.

The doors spread open. In the three seconds of light that followed, the man's face was clearly illuminated. The six rode forward.

"Thomas Fairchild!"

The paunchy man stopped and stared across the street. "That's me. Who're you—SHIT!"

"Citizens' Vigilante Council!"

Fairchild raced down the boardwalk, nearly

tripping over a stray dog that lay sleeping beside a water trough. The six mounted men took off after him.

"Help!" he called out.

Riding alongside the boardwalk, the leader of the vigilantes overtook the fleeing man and halted his horse directly in front of him where the rickety porch dropped down to bare earth. The others quickly closed in. He was trapped.

"What in hell are you guys doing?" Fairchild asked.

"Thomas Fairchild, you're a worthless gambler who doesn't deserve to walk the streets of this town!"

"No!"

"As county treasurer, you've stolen over $10,000 in public funds and wasted it all on women, whiskey and cards. You've squandered the monies of the fine citizens of Boise." The leader motioned with his free hand to his men. "Get him!"

Ten people assembled 50 yards away, watching silently as the vigilantes grabbed Fairchild and dragged him to the square where Goldrush met Whitten Avenue.

"No! God no! I haven't done anything wrong!" Fairchild frantically searched the men's eyes.

"Like hell!" the leader spat.

"You have no right!"

He broke free and ran ten feet before two vigilantes sent him sprawling to the ground.

"The rope!"

It was produced. The leader sat on his mount, arms crossed on his chest, watching as the noose was lowered around Tom Fairchild's neck and thrown over the highest branch of the ancient oak tree in the middle of the square.

"For God's sake, people, help me!" he screamed at the men and women watching from a distance.

"Save your breath, thief!" the head vigilante said. "Your stealin' days are over!"

The five men hauled him onto a horse. Bullets quenched the four kerosene lamps surrounding the square. The darkness that swallowed up the scene was soon broken by snorts and a long, agonized scream.

"Let's get the hell out! Now, men!"

The five raced to their horses. They rode out of town, joking, whooping and sending hot lead into the skies above them.

The assembled citizens turned their backs and walked away, muttering to themselves, shaking their heads.

In the public square of Boise, Idaho Territory, the county treasurer kicked and screamed, feeling the coarse hemp rope squeeze the breath from his body until he felt nothing but a long, endless drop into eternity.

Spur's brain exploded with the sound. Gunfire. He buckled on his gunbelt and looked out the window.

Nothing. Absolutely nothing but the distant sound of hooves biting into the earth. The few people he saw on the street didn't seem concerned. Maybe he'd imagined hearing the shots. Maybe he'd dreamed it.

Maybe he really did need some sleep.

Spur yawned, scratched his stubbly chin and

pushed the brownish-red hair from his eyes as he continued staring out the cracked window. If anything had happened, surely men would be reacting. But the few citizens of Boise walking the streets at that hour seemed calm, strolling along as if nothing unusual had occurred.

It must have been his imagination, Spur McCoy decided. He'd heard so many weapons discharged, had been in so many fights and had seen so much trouble in his years with the Secret Service, that it was catching up with him.

Nothing had happened out there.

The Secret Service officer groaned and felt the weariness wash over him. It had been a long ride and he was exhausted. Sleep, he told himself and stretched out on the pigeon-feather bed.

He'd have to ask the sheriff what all that was about in the morning.

CHAPTER THREE

"Missy told me what happened last night," Lacey Evans said, staring at her father as they sipped coffee in the mansion's dining room.

"Yeah." He was absorbed in the latest edition of *The Idaho Statesman*.

Around her, silver and crystal glistened. The table was set with the finest Irish linen. The plates, strewn with the remnants of their breakfast meal, were rimmed with gold.

"Yeah." Governor Evans rustled the paper.

"On his way to the stage, Geoffrey heard about it and he told Missy."

Martin Evans grunted and stared harder at an article about his opponent in the upcoming election. "So what? You shouldn't worry about things like that, darling."

"Why not? I live here, don't I?" The 18-year-old girl dabbed a lace handkerchief at the spot of strawberry jam on her chin. "Those vigilantes went and hung poor Tom Fairchild by his neck in the square. And no one tried to stop them!"

"I know, I know." Governor Evans sighed and looked at his daughter over the paper. "How could anyone? You know what they're like. If anyone tried to stand up to them they sure wouldn't be able to do it again."

The petite girl fluffed her hair and pushed back her plate. "Father, I'm worried. You keep getting all these threats against you, and those vigilantes are riding around killing whomever they please." Lacey grabbed his arm. "What happens if I wake up in the morning and you're—you're—"

Evans put the paper down and smiled at her. "They won't touch me. Besides, it isn't them I'm worried about. It has to be one of my opponents who wants to take over this territory." A smile creased the governor's face. "Someone's just trying to scare me, is all, Lacey."

She blinked her blue eyes. "I hope so. Maybe the man who's coming to see you can help, like you said."

"Maybe. That's why I sent for him. Oh, that reminds me. Missy!" he yelled toward the kitchen. "Get rid of these breakfast things and make this house presentable. We've got company coming—important company!"

The gaunt faced man stared up at Spur McCoy. "So you're some kind of government agent?"

"That's right, Sheriff MacElravie. Governor Evans called me here to secure his safety until after

the election. I'm sure you know all about the
threats against his life?"

"Sure, sure. I've seen some of the letters that
were mysteriously delivered to Evans. No way a
man could tell who sent them." MacElravie
glanced over his glasses. "Who's paying for all this?
Your visit, I mean?"

McCoy smiled. "Courtesy of the U.S. of A."

The sheriff sighed. "Good. Nothing irregular
about the money, then. That's just what Governor
Evans would need, something else for Judd
Feingold to talk about."

"This Feingold's running against the governor,
I take it. Saw some posters about him. Actually,
I saw a lot of posters." Spur crossed his arms.

"Yep. 'Course, Feingold's the type to take a
direct attack with words. It doesn't seem likely
that he'd stoop to something like that."

"I'll look into it." Spur started for the door.

"Don't you worry none about that hanging last
night," the sheriff said.

McCoy stopped and turned back to him.
"Hanging?" His voice was weak.

"Sure. Didn't you hear about it? Maybe not. The
vigilantes were busy again. Strung up Thomas
Fairchild in the public square. Lots of folks
watched him, too."

Damn, Spur thought. "I thought I heard some
unusual activity last night, but everything seemed
so normal in the streets."

"Yeah, it's happening with regularity. Fairchild's just the latest one that someone's crossed
off his list of men to kill."

"What'd he do to attract attention?"

"Fairchild was the county treasurer. He made a small salary but was out gambling every night. He'd lose $100 in 24 hours. That made some men suspicious."

Sheriff MacElravie shook his head and tasted the coffee that had been cooling on his desk. "Too weak." He took a small bottle from his desk and poured some amber colored liquid into the brew. "I heard from a reliable source that Fairchild had been stealing money from the public funds for over a year. And he lost it, every cent of it."

"How much?"

"Hard to figure. Probably around $10,000."

Spur nodded. "And you didn't take him into custody?"

MacElravie glared at him. "Don't try to tell me how to do my job! I just heard about it this morning. What am I gonna do, have a corpse sit up before Judge Mostad?"

"Of course not."

"As I figure it, the vigilantes saved me the trouble of hauling him in."

McCoy changed the subject. "With these death threats and bodies piling up, you must have your hands full."

MacElravie sipped the spiked coffee and shrugged. "Nothing I can do about the vigilantes, they're becoming the law around here."

"Can't you track them down? Round them up and press charges against them? Hell, sheriff, how many innocent men have they murdered?"

MacElravie winced. "Look, McCoy. If I did, or said, or even thunk anything against them, I'd be kicking the wind by morning." He shook his head.

"Like I said, they run this town, whether we like it or not. I value my life too much to run up against that bunch. Besides, most of their victims have been guilty of something or another."

Spur let it sink in. "I see."

The sheriff didn't seem to want to stop them.

"That isn't exactly by the book, MacElravie."

"No, siree. But it works. I do what I have to to survive." He swallowed down half of the bitter, burning liquid. "And as for Martin Evans, he don't need my help. The governor can take care of himself." MacElravie smacked his lips. "Mighty fine coffee!"

"He have friends in this town?"

"Friends? Business acquaintances, more like." He took another sip and pushed back his glasses on his nose. "You'll meet him. Judge for yourself. The governor's a powerful man, and that scares off a lot of folks. And it keeps the fellas away from that dangerous daughter of his." He raised his eyebrows and sipped. "Ah, nothing like coffee in the morning!"

"Thanks for your time, sheriff. I'll be checking in with you."

"Fine, fine. And give my regards to Evans!"

As Spur walked down Goldrush to the mansion, something bugged him. Sheriff MacElravie might be at the mercy of these vigilantes, the whole town might be afraid of them, but that didn't seem like a good enough reason to sit back and let them do whatever the hell they wanted.

Maybe the sheriff wasn't telling him everything. Maybe he liked sitting behind his desk and not taking charge. Maybe he'd grown used to having a band of wild men doing his job.

Vigilantes were bad news. Wherever they popped up they had absolute power over the local people until they were stopped. If Governor Evans hadn't hired him, Spur thought, he just might spend some time finding out who they were.

He arrived at the end of Thistledown and knocked.

"Yes?"

A pleasant-faced older woman wrapped in layers of blue and white checkered cloth stared at him.

"I'm Spur McCoy. Here to see Governor Evans?"

"And I'm Missy—answerin' the door." Her eyes were hard, lips tight. "What you here to see him about?"

As she leaned closer to him, Spur caught the fragrance of onions hanging on her clothes. "Well, ah, just who are you?"

"I already done told you!"

"Missy, Missy, really!"

A vision of white silk appeared beside the woman. "You don't have to be so careful. Do you think someone who was here to murder my father would knock on the door?" The girl turned to face him. "We meet again! I'm Lacey Evans. My father's expecting you. If you'll come this way?"

Spur took off his hat, stepped past Missy and followed Lacey. The swing of her hips nearly mesmerized him. He didn't know how old this girl was, but she was old enough.

Lacey glanced back at him. Spur realized he'd been caught and quickly raised his gaze. She laughed. "Right in there. The governor'll be with you in a minute."

"Thank you kindly, ma'am."

"Oooh, aren't you one for manners! You could teach a lot to the menfolk who come around here!" She tossed her head and disappeared through the parlor.

If she was any indication of her father, Martin Evans would indeed be able to take care of himself. Spur walked into the oak paneled room and studied the books lining the walls. Law. Astronomy. Agriculture. Mathematics. The man wasn't stupid.

A chair turned toward him, revealing a paunchy man in shirtsleeves. "You must be Mr. McCoy!"

He walked to him. "I am indeed. Good to meet you, Governor Evans."

They shook hands. Spur nearly winced at the strength of the pudgy, tall man's grip.

"I sure am glad you're here. Election day's not far away. For some reason I wanna be sure I'm still alive to see it." The robust man laughed and waddled to the bar. Wild red hair stuck straight out from his scalp as if he hadn't brushed it for weeks. "Care for a brandy, Mr. McCoy?"

"No thanks. Too early in the morning."

"I remember when it was for me, too. Before all this started." Evans smoothed out his black vest and poured an inch of brandy into a well-dusted snifter. "Maybe I shouldn't have run again."

"From what I hear, you've been doing well, and the territory's in pretty good shape. Why shouldn't you run?"

The governor sighed and swirled the alcohol in the glass. "I'm gonna level with you, McCoy, seeing as how you're here to protect me. Politicking ain't all picnics and kissing babies. Sometimes you gotta step on toes." He sniffed the brandy. "You try to give the majority what they want but the minority doesn't like it. That makes a man lots of enemies."

"What about your opponents? Could one of them be who's behind these threats?"

"Hell, I don't know. Maybe. Only one man's a real danger. That's Judd Feingold. Just moved in here last year and he's trying to take over my territory."

"Would he stoop to something like this?"

"I don't know him well enough. Maybe." He took a drink. "Hell, McCoy. I ain't exactly the most impartial man to ask. Feingold's out to ruin my life. You mark my words—Idaho will be a state soon enough, and I wanna make sure I'm still here to see it through the transition."

Spur nodded and looked around the room. "You build this place yourself?"

Martin Evans smiled. "Sure did. All my own money too, so even if that damned Feingold wins I'll stay right here. I've got some business interests in Boise and Idaho Falls." The governor drained his glass. "But I don't wanna lose at the end of a rope or with a pound of lead in my chest." He burped.

"That's understandable."

He poured another glass. "I can hire my own protection, but I need someone to oversee the whole operation. Someone who'll keep an extra

eye out for my safety. That's you." Evans glanced
at the Seth Thomas that ticked on the mantle.
"Hell, I got a meeting with the Ladies' Church
Auxiliary. Think over what I've said and see if you
can come up with any clever ways to keep the
undertaker from getting his grubby hands on my
carcass. Got that?"

McCoy grinned. "Sure. Sure, Mr. Evans." The
man was treating him like a slave.

"Good."

The young girl waltzed into the room. "Father,
I—oh, I'm sorry, I didn't know you still had
company."

"Lacey! You're worse than ever."

"Hello, Mr. McCoy. Good seeing you again "

"Good morning, Miss Evans." Spur kissed the
hand that she extended to him.

Evans stood back, watching, "You've ah, met
my daughter before?"

"Yesterday afternoon, when I came to see you,
governor."

Martin Evans smiled. "Heck, Lacey, let the poor
man get on with his business. He's got too much
to think about without your foolishness clouding
up his brain." He lifted his glass once again.

"What's so foolish about love?"

Evans spit his brandy. "Get up to your room,
girl! I know you're growing up fast but I won't
stand for such boldness in my house!"

The blonde haired girl pouted. "Okay. Be seeing
you again, Mr. McCoy?"

"Almost assuredly."

Lacey grinned. "Well then, I'll be off. I should
get out of this old dress and take a bath."

"Git, girl!"

She flounced out of the room.

"She's quite a young lady," McCoy said.

Evans looked hard at him. "Yeah. Between her and my campaign . . . ."

"What about the vigilantes?" Spur said as he followed Evans out of the study. "I realize they're a problem, but you think there's any connection between them and those letters?"

"No. I don't think so. They may be too untamed for some tastes, but all in all they're doing a good job of cleaning up this town. Besides, they wouldn't send me any letters. They'd just string me up."

"That makes sense."

"You just concentrate on keeping me in one piece. I'll see you later, McCoy!"

CHAPTER FOUR

Spur ducked as the small explosion cracked the air inside the saloon. As he rubbed his ears the bullet slammed into the far wall, plowing into a portrait of Governor Martin Evans and knocking it from its tack.

"You take that back, George!" a gravelly voice shouted.

"Hell no!" a man shouted back. "Thomas Fairchild deserved to hang! He was cheating all of us, the whole town! The whole territory! You know it as well as anyone."

"Don't tell me what I know!"

Spur peered over the table. Two men faced each other at the bar, weapons drawn. The well dressed man's Colt sent a column of blue smoke up toward the overhead kerosene lamps.

His opponent snarled. "Come on, Jackson!

You're just pissed old Fairchild won't be lining your pockets at the table ev'ry night! You never liked him, even if you did let him squire your daughter around town! You just liked his money!''

''I never saw you throw it back in his face,'' he said. ''You took it same as every other man's silver and gold. And don't you go bad-mouthin' my little girl! She took a shine to Thomas Fairchild, she did!''

''He was just using her to get to you, to get to that bank of yours, to get to your money!'' George said.

''Yeah!''

''Who called for your two bits?'' the banker asked, staring hard at the drunk beside him at the bar.

McCoy watched with interest as the pair delivered their outbursts. The recently hanged man certainly wasn't too popular, at least in that saloon.

''Come on, Jackson, forget it. Sorry I even brought the whole damn thing up. Let's just play some cards.''

A brassy-haired saloon girl put her hands on her hips and yelled at them from the stairs. ''Boys, boys, don't end things like this! A little fightin's good for business. Makes everyone drink!''

''Stay outa this, Kelly!'' George said.

''Okay. Just don't be askin' me for any more discounts!'' She lifted her hem and sauntered up the stairs. Before she'd made it halfway, a love-starved rancher had stormed after her, grabbed her waist and squeezed.

The cowboy watched the happy couple disappear, then turned back to Jackson. "You just messed that up for me real good!"

The banker laughed. "Hell, let me buy you a drink. Okay?"

"Well . . . ."

Spur returned to his seat as the apron slapped two glasses onto the oak bar. If nothing else, Thomas Fairchild had been a controversial figure. If his dirty dealings were common knowledge, anyone could have decided to clean up the problem. McCoy wasn't surprised a vigilante group had sprung up in Boise with men like him walking the streets.

"Looks like Jackson's a mite upset."

Spur shrugged at the man across the table from him. "Was this Fairchild all that bad?"

The craggy-faced man stared into his whiskey. "That's a fact. Bad from the inside out. Some say he's been stealing since he was appointed two years ago. He sure never had no trouble making ante. That made some men wonder."

McCoy nodded. "If he wasn't well-off, it would at that. So some boys around here decided to take the law into their own hands."

His drinking companion glared up at him and slightly nodded. He leaned closer to Spur. "Yep," he whispered. "Fairchild's the last bad seed in town, as far as I know. We shouldn't be hearing any more about them."

The man was afraid of the vigilantes, Spur thought. "No one's ever stood up to them? What if they made a mistake, hung the wrong man?"

"They did once. Yeah. Feller named, ah, Gilroy. Michael Gilroy. Damn fine dentist he was too, before they strung him up." The wizened man glanced both ways. "They got him a while back and killed him. Then everybody found out he hadn't done nothing, he hadn't hurt a flea. A couple teeth, maybe, but that's all."

Spur lowered his voice as well. "Then that should have been the end of them. The public should have driven them out of town, put a stop to the killing before they did it again."

"I know, I know, but folks around here—" He sighed. "Look, it ain't right talkin' about this here, in the open and all that. What's done is done. Them boys are in power in this town now and, because no one knows who they are, they're gonna stay right where they are." He narrowed his brows. "Not even the newspaper, *The Idaho Statesman,* has printed a word about the vigilantes or the mysterious killin's."

"I see." Maybe Governor Evans hadn't told him the truth. Maybe these vigilantes were getting power-happy, testing the limits of the town's tolerance, riding on the sensations of omnipotence.

" 'Course, they may not be done at that. Fairchild might not be the end."

"Why?"

The man drained his glass, swallowed, then smacked his lips. He carefully set it back on the table and looked at Spur. "Mormons," he said. "They're coming up here from Salt Lake. Lots of folks in town aren't happy to see 'em, if you know what I mean. Some of them have been forced to leave. Houses burned. Horses killed!"

"Vigilantes?"

He stared at the empty glass, mute, motionless.

Spur was certain from the man's reaction that the vigilanties were connected with the threats against Evans' life. Maybe he'd better look into them, even if the governor didn't think it was necessary.

"Look," his drinking companion suddenly said. "I don't know why in hell you'd be interested, but there's someone who may know something about these men. A woman."

Spur nodded in encouragement.

"She was the wife of that dentist I told you about. Name of Vanessa Gilroy. Lives on Maplewood, the two-story with weeds in the yard."

"Right. Thanks." Spur started to rise but the man violently grabbed his wrist.

"Get them!" he whispered.

McCoy walked out of the bar rubbing the red bruises that creased his arm, his mind fixed on his mission.

Vanessa Gilroy opened the door. The statuesque women was draped in black, from her satin bonnet to the wisps of petticoats that dragged across the floor as she let Spur into her home. With the veil covering her face and black gloves on her hands, Vanessa looked like a woman in mourning.

"I don't know why you want to talk about my husband," she said as she took a chair in her parlor. "Please."

Spur sat on the couch she motioned to and held his hat in his hands. "Just trying to gather up some facts, Mrs. Gilroy. I'm looking into the matter."

The women arched her back, lifted the veil and laughed. A fair, gloriously beautiful face glowed beneath the black lace. Flashing green eyes drilled into his; her lips, though devoid of paint, were red and full.

"Looking into the matter? I'm sorry, Mr. McCoy, but those are strange words around here. I'm not used to hearing them." She calmed herself and peeled off her left glove.

"That's quite all right. You've been through a terrible loss, and everyone in town's afraid to help you. Is that the way it is?"

She threw one glove onto the table beside her. "Close enough!" Long, beautiful fingers extricated the second sheath from her right hand. That finished, Vanessa turned to Spur. "So why on earth are you here? Why are you talking to me? I'm sorry, Mr. McCoy; I can't figure this out."

"I'm not here from the governor, and Sheriff MacElravie didn't send me."

Vanessa rubbed her fingernails together and frowned at the name.

"Let's just say I'm an interested party, interested in righting the wrong that's been done to you."

The thirty year-old woman separated her hands, unpinned the bonnet and let it fall, trailing the veil after it. Vanessa shook out the hair that she'd gathered under the hat and let it cascade to her shoulders in red ringlets that glowed in the morning sun.

"Does that bother you?" Spur asked. Something didn't seem right.

"No, no, help me all you can! I'm glad for that. But I can tell you're from out of town. Every man within fifteen miles of Boise's afraid to do anything now that the citizen's committee's watching what goes on here." Vanessa moved her chin from side to side. "I just don't think there's anything you can do."

Her eyes were bright, her lips pressed firmly together. This wasn't a woman drowning in despair, Spur thought. Had she loved her husband? Or had she accepted what had happened and the fact that nothing could be done about it?

"Leave that to me," McCoy said. "How did it happen?"

Vanessa sighed and crossed her ankles. "Six men rode up one afternoon when Michael and I were reading our Bible. He used to like to do that. Anyway, they barged in here, grabbed him and hauled him outside, yelling and carrying on like they'd eaten the wrong kind of mushrooms."

"And then?"

She wet her lips. "And then they accused him of murdering Frank Glapion, the blacksmith's son. We tried to tell them that was nonsense—Michael was in Mountain Home the day Frank turned up dead, but they wouldn't listen. They made me watch as they—they—" Vanessa turned to Spur, tears brimming in her eyes. "They did it."

"I see."

The woman angrily wiped away the drop that rolled down her cheek. "Do what you want. But I'm gonna find out who killed my husband, and I'll see that they get what's coming to them!"

Spur rose. "Maybe you should leave that to me."

Vanessa laughed. "We'll see who finds them first!" She smiled and stood. "I hate to rush you out, Mr. McCoy, but I have some things to attend to. I'm sure you understand, it's only been two weeks and there's papers to go through and everything else."

He nodded. "Okay. Thanks for the talk, Mrs. Gilroy. And if you find out anything, or have any ideas regarding the identities of the vigilantes, I'm at the Goldrush Hotel."

"Fine." She walked him to the door. "Goodbye!"

Spur stuck his wide-brimmed hat low on his head and walked out into the brilliant sunshine. Vanessa Gilroy wasn't a woman to underestimate, he decided, kicking through a maze of dying plants that flourished in her overgrown garden. Under all those tears and lace she was as tough as steel.

A woman like that would get what she wanted. Spur hoped she'd share it with him.

CHAPTER FIVE

McCoy slumped on the chair in the Goldrush dining room, exhausted. He'd been on an overnight trip with Governor Evans, who gave four speeches in as many towns in two days, jubilantly painting verbal pictures of the glories that Idaho Territory would see if he remained in office.

Even as he dug into the food he'd piled on his plate, Spur could hear the man's powerful voice blasting away at him. After hearing the same speech four times, McCoy figured he almost had it memorized.

And the people seemed receptive to Evans. Many that Spur talked with were suspicious of newcomers, "Especially that danged Feingold, with his outsider's ways." Quite a few were well aware of the *Mormon problem*, as they termed it.

The candidate's views on the Mormons seemed highly important to the people of Idaho Territory.

Evans had been straightforward—he wasn't too happy that they were moving in, but there was no way of stopping them. He went on and on about "opening your hearts to these strangers, giving them a chance to fit into the framework of the community."

During each speech, this remark had been met with boos and hisses. The governor always seemed surprised for a second, then smiled broadly. "And if that doesn't work, well, maybe they'll get tired of fighting us and move back home. That'd be the best for them and the best for us. After all, men," Evans said with a wink, "they do unnatural and ungodly things. Those boys each got three or four wives. If they move in here there'll be a painful shortage of unmarried girls!"

Cheers and shouts of approval always met this statement, and Spur was impressed by Governor Evans' ability to work the crowd that came to watch him. He was a professional, playing up to their fears.

His re-election seemed certain.

Spur had guarded the governor but nothing happened, save for a minor scuffle when some Mormons spoke up after he'd asked for questions. Their comments sparked the non-converts in the audience to action, and McCoy had to break up two fistfights before calm was restored.

Maybe Evans was only in danger at home, he thought, flaking a baked potato apart with his fork.

The bad feelings about the Mormons, and that

man's comments about them the other night in the saloon, brought the vigilantes to the forefront of his mind again. Spur sighed. He had two jobs to do in Boise.

The food quickly disappeared, giving the Secret Service agent renewed energy and vitality. Spur wiped his lip and walked outside, enjoying the cool evening air.

"Why, hello again!"

He turned to see Lacey Evans walking primly across the street, keeping her skirt well above the mud and dust that lay there.

"Good evening, Miss Evans," Spur said, tipping his hat. He took her hand and helped her onto the boardwalk that fronted the Goldrush Hotel.

The young girl stared up at him, her eyes wide under the silk bonnet that glowed a dull pink from the moon and the spill of light from the hotel.

"I hope you can help me," Lacey said.

"With what?"

"I didn't realize how late it was getting. When I left my friend's house it was already dark." She lowered her chin and pouted. "I'm afraid. I mean, I don't like to walk the streets alone at night. Could you escort me home?"

"Of course, Miss Evans."

"Thanks! And call me Lacey. Everyone calls me that. Except my father."

Spur took her arm and they walked toward Thistledown Avenue.

"What's he call you?"

"Trouble."

He chuckled. Somewhere in the distance a

rooster called, stirred by some bizarre feeling that dawn was about to break.

"Why would he call you that?" he teased. "A fine, upstanding, young girl like you?"

"I'm not a girl," Lacey said, turning to him. Her face shimmered. "I'm a woman. After all, I just reached my eighteenth birthday."

Her crinoline skirt crackled as they walked. The scent of roses drifted up from her hair. Spur held her tighter and Lacey clasped his arm. Her hand was warm. She was so small and tiny, so fragile looking. And so arousing.

Down, boy, Spur told himself. She might be of age, and she was certainly the kind of woman any man would be happy to have in his bed, but this was Lacey Evans, for God's sake. The governor's daughter!

"I love the night!" she said, looking up at the stars. "It's so cool. I just feel different after the sun goes down. Don't you?"

"Mmmm."

"I feel different tonight, like I could do anything—just anything." She swung her head farther back. "Maybe it has something to do with that moon up there."

"That moon?" Spur glanced at the pale yellow orb. "That's the same moon that's always up there. Nothing different about it."

She sighed. "Then perhaps it's the company."

Spur looked at the young girl, who squeezed his arm and laughed as they turned onto Thistledown Avenue.

"The place looks deserted," Spur said.

The bulk of the mansion loomed against the sky, dark save for a few lit windows.

"Yes. Everyone's away. Missy at her mother's—that's where she stays. My father's out doing something or other. It's amazing how he works. Why, sometimes he's out till one or two AM."

"I see."

They cleared the gate.

Lacey stopped and turned to him. "Come see the garden!" she urged him.

Spur laughed. "It's dark, Lacey."

"I know. I have a night garden!" She tugged at his arm like a child after a cookie. "Please?"

This could be dangerous. But he was used to danger—even from eighteen-year-old girls.

"Okay."

Lacey squealed with delight and took off, pulling him along with her as they raced between the manicured cherry trees and huge lilac bushes that hugged the brick walls.

"Slow down!" Spur said, feeling the old lethargy creep up his legs.

"We're almost there!"

They passed by nameless plants until the narrow path beside the mansion opened up into a vast garden. An owl that had been resting on the central sundial hooted and flew off toward the sky, its wings rasping the air.

"Alright." Lacey stopped beside a stone bench. "Close your eyes," she said, "and tell me what you smell."

"Lacey, this is crazy."

"I know, I know! Just do it. Please?"

Spur nodded and shut his eyes. The girl's hand took his. They moved forward ten feet. She pressed on his back, so McCoy stooped down.

"What is it?"

He sniffed. The scent was intoxicating, drenched with femininity and the sweetness of honey. Spur smelled it until his head grew faint.

He sighed. "I don't know, but it's frying my brain." He moved upright.

"Don't open your eyes yet! That's jasmine. Now what's this? I'll hold it up to your nose."

Lacey giggled. A bush rattled. A few seconds later Spur smelled full-blown roses.

"If I didn't know better, I say that was your hair."

He grabbed her arm and opened his eyes.

The young girl lowered the lock from his nose and glanced up at him. She smiled invitingly. "You were right. Look, Spur, we're all alone. There's no one around, and no one can see in here."

"So?"

Lacey moved closer to him until their bodies were touching. "And so? What do you think?" She gazed up at his face, lips parted, and pressed firmly against him.

Her warmth, the erotic feeling of her breasts crushing against his chest and the delightful scent of jasmine curling up around them overpowered Spur.

Old feelings began to stir inside him. "Lacey, you're beautiful. Don't misunderstand me. But you're—"

"I'm old enough!" She ground her groin against

his thighs. "I told you I'm eighteen. Since the 27th of last month."

"You're also Governor Evans' daughter."

Spur felt the primal excitement grow within him. Her body nourished it, built it up to an almost undeniable level.

"Don't think about him!" Her voice was breathy. "That old man isn't around. What he doesn't know can't hurt him."

Lacey pushed her hand under Spur's hat and scraped her fingernails across his neck. It filled him with chills.

"I can feel that thing growing down there," she said, her voice dripping with invitation. "Are you going to refuse my offer?"

Something snapped inside him. Spur moaned and took her head in his hands, gripping it, tilting it upward. "Hell, no!" he grumbled, and kissed her.

Tongues clashed. Bodies clung to each other. The earth beneath his feet seemed to shake as Spur explored her mouth. His erection strained against the corduroy pants, against the insistent pressure from her young body.

He lifted his lips from hers. Lacey threw back her head and gasped. "Oh, yes!"

"Let's go inside," he said, pulling her closer to him.

"No. Let's do it right here!"

Spur looked around. "Here?"

"Yes!"

Lacey pushed away from him. She tugged at her bonnet. The ties unravelled and she threw it onto a mignionette bush. The girl took Spur's hand, curled his fingers under the bodice of her dress and pushed them downward.

Spur went to her as the cloth ripped and fell open. He tugged at it, tearing and rending the fabric. The garden echoed with Lacey's laughter as he tore off her clothes, denuding her piece by piece, until the last petticoat and her creamy chemise lay in a heap at her feet.

"Jesus, Lacey, you're some fine woman!" he said.

"And you're some fine man!"

Her moonlight-splashed body glowed with a firefly's glory. The white shoulders, full breasts, slender waist and flaring hips were perfectly proportioned. Lacey reached for his crotch, unbuttoned his trousers and hauled them down. Her hands were experienced, Spur noted with wonder.

She lowered his drawers and smiled as the obvious proof of his arousal sprang out toward her. "I like that, Spur! I like that a lot!"

He threw back the hand that she extended toward his crotch. "You touch it and it's liable to spit at you!" he said, his voice husky. Spur quickly removed his shirt and pulled his pants off over his boots.

"So soon?"

"It isn't my doing. It's all your fault, Lacey!"

She nodded, sat on the petal-strewn earth and lowered her back. Spur stared between her upraised, parted knees. The blonde patch there drew him in. He knelt before her.

"You like my garden?" Her voice was dreamy. She circled her hips, lifting them to him.

"God, yes!"

Spur stretched out over her and fit his body between her thighs. He rubbed his erection back and forth over her opening.

"Oh!"

"Now?" he asked.

"Can't you feel how wet I am?"

"Yeah. I guess you want it."

He drove into her. Lacey gasped and puffed as he joined his body with hers. The long, slick slide was too exciting, too stimulating. He slowed his penetration, inching into her warmth, extending the timeless moment until his testicles pressed against her.

"Oh, Spur!" Lacey said, shaking her head from side to side.

"Lacey! What you do to a man!"

He kissed her, ripped his mouth from hers and sucked her right breast. The tight, wet feeling enveloped him with ecstasy, demanding action.

Spur pulled out and plunged back in. Their hip bones crashed together. He lifted his head from the groaning woman and pumped into her with short, deep jabs. The pebble beneath his toes didn't bother Spur as he pleasured her. Lacey sighed and arched her back, offering herself to him, giving him access to the most precious part of her body.

"Yes. Yes. Yes!" she chanted with each thrust.

"Lacey!"

The sound of flesh slapping against flesh broke the stillness of the garden. His groans rose with hers as they struggled together, hands clasped, mouths locked.

Staring up at him, Lacey caught her breath again and again, finally exploding into tremors and gasps, her breasts heaving up and down below him.

The increased pressure and the young woman's excitement pushed Spur over the edge. He drove blindly into her, bucking deeper, his mind whirling. The spasms, the spurts and deep release rocketed through his body. Again and again he blasted his seed into Lacey as their eyes locked and their bodies trembled.

McCoy kicked his heels as he spent himself, rustling the jasmine bush that grew above them. Fragrant white petals rained onto the panting pair as the liquor of total release dripped through their veins.

As jasmine flowers landed on Spur's head and back he kissed her again, slowing his spasmic thrusts, breathing out the paroxysms of pleasure that tore at his very being.

Lacey gathered him up in her arms, moaning against his tongue. The scent of jasmine mixed with their musk as he stopped moving and hugged her. He broke the kiss and gasped into her ear, puffing out the fine hair that lay scattered around her head.

A breeze swept through the garden, evaporating the sweat that seethed on McCoy's back. "Whew, Lacey!" he said.

"My feelings exactly, sir."

He deliberately thrust his foot into the bush,

renewing the aromatic rain and completely covering their bodies with a thick layer of gleaming jasmine flowers.

CHAPTER SIX

Vanessa Gilroy banged her thumb as she pounded the last nail into the window frame.

"Darn!" she said, sucking it, trying to soothe away the sudden pain with her lips. She put down the hammer and glanced outside. The night seemed quiet enough, but the widow knew that at any time six cowards on horseback could ride into town and snuff out a life as easily as a cigar butt.

The memories of that awful day swept through her. Vanessa choked back a sob, straightened her back and checked her appearance in the small mirror over the coatrack. Satisfied by her somber clothing, she smoothed the veil over her face, turned down the kerosene lamps and walked outside.

Some day I'll have to do something about those

weeds, Vanessa thought as they pulled at her skirt. The sheriff's office wasn't far, but she hurried down the darkened street, her leather boots scuffing through the dust. It wasn't much after eight; he should still be there. Sheriff MacElravie rarely went home before nine at night.

Vanessa Gilroy smiled beneath the black lace as she walked. She was finally doing something, not just hiding in her house, moaning about the injustice of it all. She'd wasted enough time with those womanly things. It was time for action!

The widow quickened her pace as pictures of the coming event rolled around in her mind. She was so caught up in her planning that she was surprised to find herself standing in front of the building.

She went in.

"Widow Gilroy!"

"Sheriff MacElravie, I have to talk to you." Vanessa wrung her hands. "I can't believe what I've seen!"

"What's wrong?" the lean-cheeked man asked, respositioning his thick glasses on his nose. He pushed his chair away from the desk.

"It's hard to explain. Just come with me. Please!"

"Now?"

"Yes! Before it's over!"

"Well, well," he stammered.

"Please, sheriff, you wouldn't want to miss this! It's unspeakable!"

He sighed and rose from the chair. "Alright."

They walked to her house.

"What's all this about?" Sheriff MacElravie asked as they hurried along the street.

"I was just finishing up dusting when I saw it, right out my bedroom window."

He sighed. "Saw what?"

"Saw what? A pagan wedding, that's what I saw!" Vanessa increased her pace. "There was a wedding going on in the house behind mine—you know, the old Martin place? I guess it was sold, because there was a man standing up with three women. They were getting married. *All of them!*"

"Land sakes!" MacElvravie said, huffing as he tried to keep up with the woman's strides.

"It's one thing for those Godless souls to live here, but it's another to let them do that kind of thing! We can't have unholy unions taking place in Boise, can we?"

"Absolutely not!" The sheriff touched her shoulder. "I'm mighty glad you told me about this, Vanessa."

She shrugged. "Everyone knows what you think about those Mormons. I thought you might want to see it."

"Indeed I do!"

They were both winded by the time they stood on her front porch. "Sheriff, could you take off your gunbelt and leave it out here? I don't feel comfortable with firearms inside my house."

"Sure, Widow Gilroy. I understand." He unbuckled it and let the heavy apparatus fall onto a rattan chair.

"Fine. Follow me!"

She let him in and raced up the stairs.

MacElravie trudged after her and finally walked into her bedroom. The low lamps cast a yellowish glow.

"Which window?" he asked, loosening his collar.

"That one!" Vanessa pointed to the glass beside her plain iron bed.

The sheriff went to it and peered outside. "Nothing there now. The place looks deserted."

"Really? Damn it! I guess it's over." Vanessa crossed her arms as George MacElravie turned to her. "Can you imagine something like that? Taking three wives?"

"They're un-Biblical. They bring their wicked, blasphemous ways into our own town! We can't let this thing happen!"

"Maybe they were just using the Martin house for the wedding. I couldn't see who they were from up here. I don't think it was one of the locals." She raised the veil from her face and smoothed it out over her black bonnet.

The sheriff smiled. "You did right in telling me about this, Widow Gilroy. I'll have my boys look into it. This has gone far enough!"

"Some folks say the vigilantes have gone far enough, too." Her voice was low.

He grinned at her. "What did you say?"

"You heard me, Sheriff. The vigilantes are taking over this town, killing innocent citizens!"

"Now hold on, woman! The Mormons are one thing, the vigilantes are quite another."

Vanessa laughed and turned up the flame on the wall lamp. The light that welled up in the room illuminated the sheriff's confused face.

"They're just the same. Both Godless people breaking the laws of Jesus and man alike! Wouldn't you agree with that?"

He set his jaw. "No, ma'am. No, I would not! You don't fully comprehend what you're talking about."

"Yes, I do." She sweetly smiled and lifted her left eyebrow. "And so do you. You know all about the Citizens' Vigilante Committee. More than you've told anyone."

George MacElravie stared hard at her, his left cheek twitching. "Just what are you driving at, woman? What are you trying to say?"

She closed the bedroom door and faced him again. "That you're one of them! You're one of those murdering sons of bitches!" Her fiery eyes burned into his.

He broke the stare. "Get off it, Vanessa!" MacElravie said. "That's a pile of horsedung if I've ever heard one!"

"You killed my husband! Murdered him in cold blood. Took the only man I ever loved away from me!" she screamed.

"Stop it! Act like a grown woman. Have you gone out of your mind?"

"No. You did, the minute you ganged up with them, the moment you slapped that horse and left my husband dangling by his neck from the limb." She ripped off her hat and veil. "Admit it! You're one of them!"

The sheriff planted his feet on the floorboards, his hands at his sides. "So what if I am?" he asked, smiling. "Just what the hell are you gonna do about it? I'm the law in Boise, Vanessa! I'm the goddamned sheriff!" He pounded on the star pinned to his chest.

She snickered. "The law? Or *lawless!*"

"Widow Gilroy, you shut your mouth and keep it shut!" MacElravie reached for his right thigh. His fingers closed around empty air.

Vanessa poked a hand into her skirt pocket. "It's out on the front porch. Remember?"

"You bitch!" He lunged at her.

Cold steel flashed up in her hand. The sheriff stumbled backward out of her reach.

"Hell! Where'd that thing come from?"

Vanessa grinned and stabbed the air with the knife. "You're not going to kill another innocent victim, George!"

"Now, now, Widow Gilroy," MacElravie said. Glistening drops poured down his face, slipping his glasses nearly off their perch. "Don't go and do anything stupid with that thing. Give it here!"

"I'll give it to you, like you gave it to my husband!"

Vanessa advanced on him, gripping the Bowie knife with a firm hand, her arm strong, muscles tight.

The sheriff backed toward the door. "What the hell are you doing?"

"Justice!"

His hands scrambled at the doorknob behind him. His face tightened as he tried to turn it.

"I thought of everything. Your revolver's outside. Door's locked. Windows nailed shut. You aren't going anywhere, sheriff!''

He flattened against the oak door, the muscles in his neck popping out as the deadly steel blade closed in on him.

''Jesus, no!'' he whispered, frozen in disbelief.

''Yes!''

Closer.

''You wouldn't really—''

Vanessa Gilroy grunted and plunged the knife into his chest. She smiled at the satisfying crack of bones and the disgusting sound of ripping tissues as it slid into the sheriff's body.

The man's face contorted. ''No! God, no!''

Before his hands touched the knife the widowed woman pulled it out and rammed it back in, digging into the murderer's heart, ripping and tearing the big pump.

The sheriff collapsed, clutching the knife buried in his chest, gurgling and staring up at her in shocked surprise. Eerily wet sounds issued from his throat.

''You killed him!'' she said, and sat on the floor before him, staring at the stain that slowly spread on his checkered shirt front.

His chin slumped to his chest.

Vanessa Gilroy patiently waited, even hummed a hymn as she watched the man die. The bleeding finally halted, the spasms stopped shooting through his form. Sheriff MacElravie was finally dead.

The smell of blood rose up from his body, sickening her, but the widow's jubilation overcame the urge to vomit. She yanked out the knife and wiped it clean with a monogrammed handkerchief that her husband had given her when they were courting.

"Michael, this one's for you," she whispered to the spirit that she felt hovering around her, and unlocked the bedroom door.

Ten minutes later she'd hauled the sheriff down the stairs. Vanessa stared at the grandfather clock that ticked comfortingly near the fireplace. Four hours to wait.

She did some needlepoint, returning to the seat cushion she'd been working on lately. Once in a while she glanced over her close work at the lifeless form that lay on her parlor floor and smiled. Everything was finally going her way.

At midnight, Vanessa Gilroy went behind her house and hitched her old mare to the carriage. She drove up to her front door and hauled the dead man into the conveyance, silently thanking her father for working her so hard, remembering how he'd forced his daughter to help out with the boy's chores after her brother had died in an accident on the farm.

She calmly drove three streets from her home. Dressed in black, the veil covering her face, no one could tell who she was even if they did see her. But she met no one. The houses and the streets were dark.

The woman kicked and rolled Sheriff MacElravie's body onto the dirt, thrilling to the dull sound as it hit the earth. That done, she slowly drove home, put the horse in the small shelter and wiped up the stains that covered the parlor floor. Next, she cleaned up her bed-room.

Vanessa took the soiled cloth and the handkerchief downstairs and threw them into the fireplace. Her clothing soon followed it, every stitch until she stood naked. The shivering woman lit a taper from the wall sconce and lit the pile of blood-smeared clothing.

As the flames lapped the stiff black material and rose up the chimney, destroying the evidence of what she'd done, Vanessa laughed until the vivid memories of her beloved husband flooded through her. Her triumph dissolved with the tears that splattered onto the polished hardwood floor.

"Did you hear what happened last night?" Governor Evans shouted as Spur McCoy walked into his library. "Sheriff MacElravie is dead! Stabbed through the heart and dumped onto the street!"

Spur took off his hat. "No, I hadn't heard."

He'd been cautious about facing the man the morning after, but Evans seemed oblivious to what may have happened between McCoy and his daughter.

"Jesus, I can't believe it!"

"The vigilantes?" Spur guessed.

Evans turned to him. "Hell, no!" He sighed and rubbed his forehead. "I don't know. Everything's all messed up now."

"Did anyone see anything?" Spur asked, remembering the ineffectual sheriff. "Was this another public execution like all the others?"

"No." The governor went to his brandy. "Nothing like it. This wasn't them vigilantes. It couldn't have been. They hang men, they don't stab them. And they make sure everyone sees them ride into town. You can't miss them."

"Maybe they've changed their methods. Maybe hanging got boring after awhile. You string up three or four men and where's the excitement?"

Evans splashed some liquor into a glass and downed it in one swallow. "I don't know."

"Seems like you're not the only one in town who might not wake up in the morning. Lots of murders going on here," he pointed out.

"You think I don't know that? But I'm not gonna cancel that big speech I have scheduled for this afternoon. Nothing's gonna scare me away from meeting the voters!"

"Okay. I'll plan security for it." Spur mulled over the situation. "That's the one in the church. Right?"

Evans nodded and took another drink.

"Fine. I'll see you there at noon. Meanwhile, think I'll see what I can find out about the sheriff's murder."

"You do that, McCoy! Find the bastard who killed him!" He refilled his glass.

As he left, Spur was surprised at the governor's reaction to MacElravie's death. He'd breezed through the other recent murders without a care, but this one seemed to have gotten to him. Why?

He shook his head and wandered over to the saloon. That's usually a good place to gather information in a hurry, and the whole town should be buzzing with the news—if, indeed, the vigilantes hadn't killed the man.

What had the sheriff done?

When the man was gone, Governor Evans sucked up another glassful of brandy and sat at his desk. The burly man slammed his fist onto its slick surface, almost enjoying the pain that ripped up his arm.

This was unthinkable, he raged in his mind. Absolutely unthinkable! Who the hell had killed him?

He stood and paced back and forth, thinking. The longer he waited, the more questions he'd have. He walked out of his house and saddled up his fastest horse. He had some people to talk to!

CHAPTER SEVEN

Vanessa smiled, thinking over what she'd done last night. The incident was fresh in her mind—the glorious feeling of ultimate triumph. Victory was sweet.

She had feigned shocked surprise when she'd heard of the sheriff's murder on her way to the dry goods store earlier that morning. It seemed that was the biggest thing that had happened to Boise in recent years.

Doubt crept up inside her, boiling like a teapot kept too long on the flame. No one had apparently connected John MacElravie's death with the vigilantes. That had been her mistake. If she could find a way to make it seem like they had done the killing it would serve them right, Vanessa thought. It could have maintained her innocent appearance.

Widow Gilroy wondered what the other

vigilantes thought when they heard that one of their own was dead. She wished she could see their faces.

The woman stared into her own eyes in the hallway mirror. The memories swept over her again, twisting and turning through her mind like a prairie storm. The widow again felt the hands biting into her shoulders and neck as two men forced her to watch. She remembered her husband's tortured words to her just before it happened. Once again, she saw him hanging like a dead chicken from the tree.

Vanessa had watched every second. When the horse had bolted forward, when the rope had snapped tight, when Michael Gilroy had screamed as he was suddenly suspended in midair, she had sworn vengeance against those men. The vivid recollections of that hideous day possessed her.

One down, Vanessa thought. Those words soothed her. She smiled at her reflection and sat in her beloved rocker. One down, and five to go.

When it was all over, maybe she'd be able to sleep all through the night unhaunted by the eerie sound of hemp rope creaking as it swayed back and forth and fresh wood snapping under the weight it bore.

Maybe.

Jake Bancroft pushed his boots into the braided rag rug. "Come on, Candra; you know that's our mission! That's why we're here in the first place. I don't like Boise any more than you do, but we're doing the work of the Lord."

The twenty-year-old woman stopped stirring and set down the wooden bowl. "Jake, I realize that. But how much can we do if they kill us?"

"Candra, really!" Maureen said as she sat near the fireplace, stroking Lois' fine blonde hair. "They aren't savages, you foolish girl. They're human beings."

"You're quite right, wife of mine. Misguided, unenlightened—but human."

"But they aren't God-fearing souls. They don't follow our ways! They don't even understand us!" Candra gasped and pushed the spoon into the cornbread dough. "All we have is the Stones across the street and our faith to sustain us. I'm just not sure that's enough."

"It is, child, it is!" Jake kissed her cheek. "The Lord will protect us!" He stepped back and frowned at her. "And I'll talk to Governor Evans again. He wasn't pleased with my words, but he will hear me!"

Candra stared across the room at her sister wives. As usual, Lois and Maureen were having a great time. The two women were inseparable. They met her gaze with laughter and smiles. She turned back to the counter, gripped the wooden spoon and stirred the stiff mixture.

Jake wiped his hands on his pants. "And besides, the election's coming up. Maybe Judd Feinhold will win. He's sympmathetic to our cause."

"Candra! You aren't losing faith, are you?" Maureen said. "I'd hate to lose you as a sister!"

"I'm not your sister," she said bitterly into the dough. "I'm Jake's wife."

"And so am I."

He walked to the fireplace. "Girls, do everything you can to bolster up Candra's faith. I have some chores to attend to."

"Yes, husband!" the two chanted in unison.

"They hate us!" Candra said. "They hate us enough to kill us!"

Jake hesitated at the door, shook his head and walked outside.

Candra saw Maureen's mocking face in the bowl and stabbed it with the spoon, slicing her perfect cheekbones with huge gashes.

Everything had been fine. She'd just converted and Jake had married her, saving the young girl from a life of lonely darkness. They had built a house and she had enjoyed caring for him.

Then it had begun. She'd heard all about polygamy, of course, but Jake had never mentioned it in relation to them. One day, he brought a young woman home with him and introduced her as his next wife.

The shock had been so severe that Candra just smiled and talked with the stern-faced woman. Jake had let her sit down to dinner with them that night. At first, Maureen had been as friendly as she could under the circumstances.

After a while Candra noticed a distinct change. The woman kept her sentences short and clipped. Her smiles were less frequent and she clutched Jake's hand under the table.

She's jealous of me, Candra had thought. Jealous of the first wife! Maybe she could drive the woman away, make her so mean and ugly that Jake would forget all about her.

It hadn't worked. They'd been married and soon the bitch was sharing her bed every night. Candra fought back tears as she remembered lying beside them, shaking back and forth with the bed, forcing her head harder into her pillow to block out the revolting sounds of their couplings.

By the time Lois, too, had moved in, Candra was beyond caring about it anymore. Everything about their religion was right except this. It wasn't natural. It was evil.

But there was nothing she could do. She waited it out and eventually grew to like Lois, the short, soft-voiced woman who was the exact opposite of Maureen. They even stitched together and talked about future babies, though none of them had any on the way.

But Maureen hadn't warmed to her. A year after their nuptials the woman was cold and harsh with Candra, exploding over the tiniest thing.

Now, here in Boise, she couldn't put up with it anymore. She'd stayed with Jake because she loved him, and had realized that sharing his love was better than being alone. But now the danger—the whispered comments on the street, the ugly rumors spreading around town about them, the real anger that showed in the people's faces—forced her to face the truth. She couldn't face a whole lifetime of Lois and Maureen. She couldn't live in a place that hated her and everything for which she stood.

"You gonna beat that dough to death?" a voice cut into her thoughts.

Candra turned and stared at Maureen, who frowned at her.

"You know better than that. You keep that up and that cornbread'll be flatter than your chest!"

She hurled the bowl at the wall, flinging it with the hatred that surged through her body. It crashed against the bricks and slid to the floor with a dull rattle. "You bit—"

"Maureen!" Lois said. "You promised to be nice to our sister wife."

"Dear, sweet Lois!" Maureen bent down and kissed her head. "I never said such a thing. How can I be nice to a woman that hates me?"

"She's still new. She doesn't understand everything about our faith." Lois sat up and smoothed down her apron.

Maureen laughed. "She just wants Jake for herself. She thinks she's woman enough for him!"

Candra fought back the words, biting her index finger as her body racked with silent sobs.

"Oh, did I make you cry again?" Maureen asked with mock sympathy. "Get used to it, sister wife!"

"Come on. Let's play." Lois snuggled up to the woman.

Candra watched in revulsion as Maureen cupped the younger woman's breast and squeezed it.

"Don't you want to join in?" Her voice was wicked.

"No!"

Candra ran from the room and collapsed on the bed. As she cried she felt the four distinct impressions that creased the huge feather mattress, and rolled into the familiar one that hugged her body every night while Jake wrapped his arms around Lois and Maureen.

"Your speech sounded better than ever," Spur said as the governor led him up to the front door.

"Yep! Talk's one of my strong points." Evans reached for the knob. "Not another one!" He bent and retrieved the piece of paper that had been tacked to the front door. "Another note!" He shook his head and let Spur into his mansion.

In the library, Governor Evans unfolded it and laid it on his desk. Spur bent over his shoulder to read it. The block letters were written in blue ink:

WARNING! EVANS, YOU DON'T LISSEN.
LEAVE TOWN ORR WE BURIE YOU!

"I see he hasn't learned how to spell yet," McCoy said. "It seems to be close to the last one."

"Identical in intent," Evans said. He scratched his chin. "You think I should be worried about this? Nothing's happened to me. I'm as healthy as a bird!"

"I don't know. In situations like this it's best to act as if the threat was real. If it isn't, it doesn't matter. If it is, you're prepared." He eased into the leather-upoholstered chair in front of the governor's desk.

"I know all that," he said with a snarl. "That's why I sent for you! I just want your gut feeling on this." The big man stared down at the note.

Spur sighed. "I don't know. All the vigilante activity in town might have been inspirational."

"How so?"

"A few citizens righting wrongs could set a trend. Others could take actions against those they assume have acted against them. Maybe someone's toes still feel the pressure from your feet."

"Yeah, but why wait? This man hasn't tried anything directly against me. Sure, he's sent notes and broken a few windows, but that's it."

"He's nervous. Threatening to do something is a hell of a lot easier than doing it."

Evans shook his head. "Maybe I don't need you after all, McCoy." He looked at the bottle of brandy in the corner of the room. "I think this guy's talking big. It's probably one of Lacey's would-be suitors that I turned away at the door."

"That's a possibility," Spur admitted. "But I'm here. I might as well stay in town and look into things."

"Fine with me!" Evans rose.

"Governor, think you could give me some ideas?"

"Ideas?" he asked, mystified.

"Yeah. Can you think of anyone in town who's been upset with you? Someone you've tangled with in the past, bad enough to make him want to do something like this?" Spur McCoy tapped the note.

"Well, sure! There's Judd Feingold, my opponent." Evans pinched his brows. "And, of course, the Mormons never have settled well with me. There's only two families left in Boise." He thought. "Jake Bancroft and I had some words a few months back, right after he moved in with his family on Plainfield Way. He didn't seem to like me. And the feeling was mutual, I might add."

"A Mormon and a politician. Well, it's something," Spur said. "Thanks for your help."

"I doubt it'll do you any good, but you're welcome to try." He pushed out his hand.

They shook.

"If by some miracle I do get a man to confess to writing these letters I'll surely let you know, Governor Evans."

"I'd appreciate that. Well, I'm sure you know the way out."

Spur did, and walked there quickly, trying to avoid a danger that lurked in the stately halls of the mansion. But before he reached the front door soft hands grabbed his waist, yanked him back and twisted him around.

"You wouldn't leave without giving me a kiss, would you?" She pressed up against him.

"Lacey!" Spur moved back and glanced at the library. "Keep it down, okay?"

The girl pouted but spoke softly. "You didn't keep it down last night." She eyed him and twirled a curl of blonde hair around a finger.

"I know. I just don't want your father to stain his carpet with my blood!"

"Didn't you like it?" she asked, flapping her lashes over widened eyes.

"Of course I did! We can't talk here. Come on, Lacey; let's go outside."

She happily followed him, smiling and bouncing in her plain blue dress. Out in the bright sunshine

Spur grinned in spite of himself at her youthful glee.

"As much as I hate it, I don't think we should see each other when your father's around. You know why."

She nodded. "If he even suspected, he'd fix it so that you couldn't ever love me again. And that wouldn't be any fun for me at all!"

"You have a way with words, Lacey," Spur said, and kissed her cheek. "I have to be going. See you later."

She grabbed his shirt. "When?" she insisted.

"Soon. Ah, soon. When I have the time and the governor's busy with something else—somewhere else."

"Alright. I'll try to wait until then!"

Spur wrested himself from her grip and walked toward the eagle-topped iron gate.

CHAPTER EIGHT

When he got to Plainfield Avenue, Spur soon realized it wouldn't be difficult to find this Jake Bancroft. The street was much like any other in such towns—houses spaced well apart with plenty of empty land between them.

But as he walked beside them he saw that most had been boarded up. On others, front doors stood open, swinging back and forth in the hot breeze. Tattered curtains fluttered from broken windows.

Up ahead, two blackened mounds of wood showed the effects of devastating fires. McCoy stopped and studied them. The blazes had been so recent that the street was still peppered with ash, and the dank smell of destruction hung around them.

Plainfield must have been the unofficial Mormon Way, Spur thought as he moved on. If all the houses had once held Mormon families, they'd had hard times in Boise. At least Governor Evans had been honest about his feelings concerning them.

Spur finally found a freshly-kept, brightly painted two-story clapboard house. The Bancrofts? He knocked and the door soon opened.

A large-boned man peered out at him. "Yes?" His voice was wary.

"I'm looking for Jake Bancroft, but I don't know the address."

"You got him."

"Good. Mr. Bancroft, I'm with the U.S. Government, looking into problems in this town of yours."

Bancroft laughed. "Heck, Boise isn't my town!" He didn't open the door farther.

"Can I come in?"

"How do I know you're not one of those vigilantes?" Bancroft asked.

"I'm not. Besides, from what I hear, they work together. Six men." He gestured behind him. "I'm alone and I'm not wearing a kerchief mask. Okay?"

The man mulled it over and nodded. "Fair enough. Come on in."

Spur stepped into the house. It was a stark, brightly lit place with simple furnishings—hand made tables and chairs, two spinning wheels, a loom and a small shelf holding leather-bound books. The scent of cooking apples filled the air.

He heard laughter and feet shuffling in an adjoining room.

"Sorry about that rude welcome," Jake said, turning to him after closing the door. "But I have to be careful these days. Too many people in town I can't trust. Starting with Governor Evans."

"I understand," Spur said.

"Have a seat."

Spur did.

Jake paced. "I truly don't understand what these folks are afraid of! My family's not out to rape, loot or kill. All we want is a quiet, peaceful life."

"And spread the word about your faith. Right?"

"Sure, of course."

"These people aren't afraid of you, Bancroft. They're afraid of change. You represent new ideas, new ways of thinking. It threatens them and their own faith."

He lowered his head. "I know. But those—those—" He shook his head. "They think it gives them the right to burn down houses and force my people out of town!"

"That must not set well with you," McCoy probed. "All this anger and violence directed toward your people. Has anything happened to you or your family?"

Jake softened his voice. "Yes. Last week I was walking out of the general store. Someone slammed the butt of his pistol into my neck. When I turned around he was gone—just vanished." He rubbed the tender spot and winced. "I never told my family about it. Last thing I want is for them to worry about me."

"Have you received any threatening letters?"

The Mormon stared hard at him. "Matter of fact,

I have. Just yesterday. Candra found one shoved under the door.''

"Can I see it?"

''I burned it up soon as I read it. It was written in big letters, something about 'we don't like your stink. Go back where you came from.' '' Bancroft rubbed his palms together. ''First one we got, but the other families—the Warners, the Greenaways—they got letters. Two days later their houses were torched. I don't mind saying I'm nervous.''

The words were true, Spur realized. This wasn't the kind of man who'd send notes to Governor Evans. Bancroft was more than nervous. He was scared, afraid for his life.

That ruled him out.

''Look, I don't know who you are, but if you can do anything to calm these people down I'd—''

Spur grunted. ''Afraid there's not much I can do. But I am looking into the vigilantes, trying to find out who they are. They're behind all the persecution. Right?''

Bancroft nodded so vigorously his lower lip wobbled. ''Yes, sir! Those men are crafty. No one knows who they are and they won't try to put a stop to them.'' He shook his head. ''Boise sure is different than Salt Lake.''

''You could always go back.''

Jake smiled. ''That's just what they want, isn't it? No. We can't. It's our mission to bring the word to these people. It doesn't matter if they want to hear it or not. Some will, and that'll make all this worthwhile.''

"Those are brave words, Bancroft."

As Spur rose from the chair he saw three women standing in the kitchen door, staring at him with wide eyes. They ranged in age from about 20 to 35, all unique ladies, simply dressed in non-provocative clothing.

"My wives," Bancroft said, his eyes shining. "Come on, girls. Get back to work!"

They frowned and disappeared.

"You must be some kind of man," Spur said, grinning.

Bancroft puffed out his chest. "They're a handful, alright. But we get along."

"Thanks for your help." McCoy walked out.

Halfway down Plainfield, Spur heard rapid footsteps behind him. He turned and saw a young woman racing toward him, her skirts flying in the air.

"Wait!" she said desperately.

As the woman neared him, he recognized her as the youngest of Jake Bancroft's wives. She panted and clutched her chest. "I have to talk to you."

"Fine, Mrs. Bancroft. Let's talk."

"Not here." She whipped her head around, sending her brown pony tails flying. "I snuck out the kitchen door. Jake doesn't know I'm gone. Let's go into town."

They went quickly. Spur tried to take her arm but the young woman brushed away his hand. Curious, he walked with her onto Goldrush. "Where now?"

She glanced both ways and shrugged. "Your hotel?"

"Mrs. Bancroft!" Spur said in surprise.

"The name's Candra," she said, her cheeks coloring. "And I'm only thinking about my safety. Let's go!"

Two minutes later, Spur closed the curtains and turned up the lamps. Candra Bancroft sat in the rickety chair that she'd thrust under the doorknob. In the soft light she looked older than her years—eyes low and dark, lips firmly set, shoulders slumped with defeat.

"What's the problem, Candra?" he asked, standing before her.

"My husband. And his other wives." She bit her lower lip. "I just can't stand it any more. Jake refuses to take us back to Salt Lake. He seems to think we'd all be better off dead or losing everything than face the church elders there, admitting defeat."

Spur nodded. "Your husband's faith is very strong. Unbreakable."

"I know. And so are his other wives." The word was harsh, strained. She looked up at him, raised the corners of her mouth and blinked. "But that's behind me now. I'm leaving town, going to Pocatella where I have friends. It's the only thing I can do, and I need your help."

"Sure. Can't you just divorce your husband?"

Candra rolled her eyes. "There's no time! We've got a few days at most before they run us out of town. If they burn the house and we're all asleep in it . . . ." The words trailed. She clutched her shoulders and stared at a spot on the wallpaper behind Spur's shoulder. "I can't wait for that to happen. Maureen and Lois—my husband's other wives—won't come with me. I tried to talk them into it but they're stubborn. So here I am.''

''What can I do?''

''I checked yesterday when I bought eggs. The stage leaves for Pocatella in the morning at dawn. I just need a place to stay tonight.''

''No problem. You can sleep here.''

Her face melted with relief. ''Thank you, Mr.— Why, I don't even know you're name!''

''McCoy. Spur McCoy.''

''I hope I won't put you out,'' Candra said, swinging her leg.

''Not at all. It won't be the first time I've slept on the floor.''

She smiled. ''You—ah—you wouldn't have to do that.'' She looked directly into his eyes.

Spur smiled wonderingly at her.

''Mr. McCoy, I've been married for a year now. For the last six months I've slept alone. Sure, three other people were in bed with me, but I was *alone*. Do you understand what I'm saying?''

He smiled. ''Yes.''

She stood and walked to the window. Candra Bancroft ran her fingers up and down the green fringe that edged the curtains. ''A woman has certain, well, needs. Her husband should fulfill them for her while he's fulfilling his.''

''That's the way it's supposed to work.'' He looked at the back of her dress. She was a strange woman.

''But when a man has three wives, one of them can fall through the cracks of his needs.''

He grunted affirmatively.

Candra unfastened her pony tails and let her lightly curled brown hair fall to her shoulders. She ran her hands through it until it shone in the yellow lamp light.

"I'm only human." She fumbled with something in front of her.

"Yes. You are that." He enjoyed the game she played with him.

"So it's only natural that when a handsome man walks into an unfulfilled woman's home, that she might . . . ."

"Perfectly natural."

She shifted her hips. "And when she's alone with him in his hotel room, shouldn't she . . . ."

"Uh-huh."

Candra turned around. Her cotton dress lay unbuttoned to the waist. She slipped it off her shoulders. Spur watched in fascination as it slid off her body with a hypnotic grace, slowly revealing her firm, rounded form. No undergarments veiled her beauty. When the dress touched the floor she was totally naked.

"Mr. McCoy, you don't know how long I've waited for a man like you!" She held out her arms. "Please. Now. Just do it! I need it so bad!"

The catch in her throat, her stunning nudity and the desperation in her eyes made him kick off his boots. His crotch pounded as he yanked off his socks and removed his shirt.

Candra silently watched him, looking into his eyes as he undressed. Then, bare and erect, he walked to her. Spur's penis stabbed her midsection before his hands fastened around her shoulders. She groaned at the erotic contact, at the closeness of him, and buried her face in his chest hair.

McCoy lifted the whimpering woman and laid her gently on the bed. Candra automatically spread her legs and thrust her hand between them, probing, flicking back and forth, pleasuring herself. "Please. Please!"

He didn't hesitate. Drunk on the young woman's musk, he entered her as gently as he could, pushing until their bodies were locked together at the waist. Candra moaned and tossed her head as he pumped.

"Faster. Faster!"

Grunting, he obeyed her animalistic command, gazing into the eyes of the woman who bounced below him. She rammed her hips up to his, meeting his driving thrusts with ever increasing urgency.

The old bed squeaked with their rhythm. Flesh slapped against flesh. Candra opened her lips, strangled out a cry and slapped a hand over her mouth. She shuddered with supernatural violence, twisting and thrashing under him as pleasure rocketed through her body.

Her contractions made his groin boil. Spur plunged faster into her, pistoning his hips. Candra rolled through a second and third climax until he lost control and joined her in a malestrom of erotic ecstasy.

The mattress came alive, bucking and buckling beneath them as their slick bodies shook together. A pure, sweet howl whistled through Spur's ears.

The moment infinitely stretched out, extending, lengthening with each powerful burst deep inside her.

Candra finally gasped and lay still below him, taking his last few pumps before he collapsed on top of the young woman. She clasped her hands around his wet back and puffed.

"I mean, it's only natural, isn't it?"

Spur mumbled something in her hair.

CHAPTER NINE

Spur did see Candra Bancroft safely onto the stagecoach the next morning. The young woman left everything behind in the dust that rose in the air behind the departing vehicle. As he watched it surge out of town, the horses fresh and eager to be out on the trail, Spur hoped she'd find her peace somewhere, sometime. And he was happy he'd given her some comfort during her last day in Boise.

Scratching an annoying itch on his chin, Spur straightened his hat and wandered down Goldrush. No reason to see the governor today, he decided, but he should let the service know he'd changed his plans. McCoy sent a telegraph to General Halleck informing him that the vigilantes were now his main targets.

He turned toward the hotel. Time for breakfast.

* * *

Just after sunset, five men rode into town,
kicking their horses into full-out gallops. Women
screamed and ran onto the boardwalk. Well fed
boys who had been playing with pop-guns, aiming
at tin can targets, shouted at each other in joy as
they hid behind water barrels. Horses tied up at
the hitching posts before the stately houses
whinneyed in response to the neighs of their new
equine friends.

Every man who heard them coming, who saw
their careless, power-drunk entrance into Boise,
wondered who they were behind their masks. And
if they were the next to be killed.

They rode abreast, spanning Goldrush, forcing
carriages and buggies to turn aside to let them
through. As soon as they'd passed, the street
returned to normal. People went back to their
everyday lives, willfully crushing all memories of
the vigilantes.

One dark clad figure watched in silence as the
five men rode relentlessly down Goldrush. He
hovered in a dark corner, moving the muzzle of
a rifle in the street dust, waiting.

The five turned onto Plainfield and halted
outside a house. They bunched together,
whispering.

"You got the kerosene and rags?" one asked.

"Yep."

"You know what to do!"

All but their leader dismounted. Cloth was
soaked with the deadly liquid. Suitable rocks were
found, tested for proper weight and wrapped with

the rags. Ends were tied to ensure they wouldn't fly off. In a minute, all was ready.

"No warning!" their leader said to them from his mount as he was handed one of the deadly packages. "Do it! Start the circle of fire. These heathens'll burn in hell; we're just giving them a head start!"

One vigilante ran around the house with a can of kerosene, pouring a trail of the deadly liquid on the sun dried plants and weeds. When he'd surrounded the structure, he rejoined the others.

Three matches were lit and thrown onto the ground. The kerosene quickly lit, rising up in a curtain of flame that extended around the house.

More matches were lit and touched to the rag-wrapped rocks until they burst into flames. The men hurled them at the house. Three crashed through windows. Two others landed on the ground and were quickly quenched.

Soon, five more rocks broke the silence. Light grew inside the house. The four men mounted up and rode down Plainview as the unholy inferno behind them exploded in a sea of brilliant destruction.

As they passed another abandoned house, gunfire rang out. One of the vigilantes howled and gripped his arm, nearly unseating himself.

"Damn! I'm shot!"

"Badly?" their leader called to him as they continued racing out of town.

"Don't think so but it hurts like shit!"

The man searched the area with his eyes. "They're long gone by now. Ride on, men! We've done our work!'' he yelled above the sounds of twenty hooves pounding into the dirt.

They left the last house behind them and rode over open countryside for two miles before slowing their horses and looking back.

A house on Plainfield lit up half the town.

''No more Mormons!'' the leader of the Citizens' Vigilante Committee yelled.

The men joked with each other as they pulled the kerchiefs from their faces. The wounded man clutched his leaking forearm and stuffed the kerchief in his back pocket.

They rested their horses and themselves before heading back into town from five different directions with five different stories.

Another victory for the vigilantes.

''Mr. McCoy! You are looking fit this morning,'' Vanessa Gilroy said as she approached him.

''Don't know how.'' He stared at her as she approached him. The widow had given up her black attire; she was wrapped in yellow crinoline.

''Bad night?''

''It was a strenous one. I got together a search party for the vigilantes. I actually had two men agree to help—they were fed up with them. We didn't find anything but tracks leading out of town that split up and led back into Boise.'' He snarled. ''And, as usual, no one had anything useful to say to me.''

''Somebody must know something,'' Vanessa said, retying the bow beneath her chin. ''But they're scared. There has to be four or five wives wondering why their husbands came in so late last night, but they'd never dare to connect that fact with what happened to the Bancrofts." She shook her head and squinted up at him. "Will you have lunch with me?"

"Sure. I haven't eaten all morning."

"Then it's time. I know a wonderful restaurant right down the street."

They walked there.

"Have you uncovered anything about the vigilantes?" Spur asked.

"I don't know for sure. I'd hate to accuse the wrong men."

"Hmmmm." She was stalling, Spur thought. But why?

"I did hear that some folks around town think that Sheriff MacElravie was one of them."

He looked at her in surprise. "Where'd you hear that?"

"I don't know. Something someone said during quilting yesterday. Course, we'll never know now that he's dead."

"He did seem to be a little too happy to let them run this town for him."

"And he never did a thing to find the men who killed my husband." Vanessa shook off the memories. "But let's not think about that now. We're here."

She led him into the small, darkly lit restaurant. They sat at a table in the corner. Appetizing smells laced with garlic and tomatoes steamed from the central rear door. Two couples sat digging into plates of food and glasses of wine.

"Nice place," he said.

Linens covered the tables. The wall sconces dripped with cut crystal, and the silverware gleamed in the soft light.

"Reminds me of Philadelphia—I mean, what I think Philadelphia would be like. It's a little bit of civilization in this uncivilized place." She unfolded her napkin and placed it on her lap.

Spur followed suit. "You come here often?" he asked.

"Not since my husband—not for quite a while." She leaned closer to him. "I didn't bring you here for the food, Mr. McCoy."

"Then what?"

"In a few seconds, a man will walk out from the kitchen. I'll bet you a glass of wine he'll have a hurt arm."

He studied her. "I'm not the gambling type, Vanessa. What are you up to?"

Before she could answer a short, dark man emerged from the kitchen.

"Mrs. Gilroy!" he said expansively, smiling and holding his hands out as if to embrace her from across the room. "I am honored by your presence, as usual," he said in a thickly accented voice. The man's right shirtsleeve was pushed up, and a white bandage circled his forearm.

"Thank you; you're too kind." Her voice was sweet. "What happened to your arm, Sam?" Vanessa asked.

The restaurateur rubbed the white bandage and ruefully grinned. "A foolish accident, I am afraid. I chop onions, I chop myself." The short

Italian grinned and placed his hands on the table. "Maybe I think about you when I do that? Not think about work?"

Vanessa laughed. "Sam Delmonico, you're an old tease. Bring us some steaks. Rare. And a bottle of your finest red wine. Okay?"

"Anything. Anything for you, my dear!"

When he'd disappeared she grabbed Spur's sleeve. "What did I tell you?"

"So he's a lousy cook. Or he isn't very careful."

Vanessa shook her head and moved her chair beside his. "Didn't you hear the stories? Someone fired a rifle last night as the vigilantes rode out of town. Sam Delmonico didn't cut himself; he was wounded after burning down the Bancroft place—and them!"

"You can't know that!" Spur said. "It could be a coincidence."

"Of course! That's why I wanted you to see for yourself." She paused. "But I hadn't seen Sam for weeks. There was no way I'd know he'd hurt himself in the kitchen." Vanessa stared at him.

"But you knew he was shot?"

"Yes. Yes! When we were all crowding around this morning, watching them pulling out the—the bodies—this Mormon woman said she saw the whole thing, the fire, the man getting shot. They live right across the street, after all! And she said the man was short. I just put two and two together. Most of the fellas in this town are big mountains of men."

He mulled it over. "You sure you didn't hire someone to take a potshot at the vigilantes last night?''

"How could I know they were going to attack the Bancrofts? Be reasonable, Spur!"

"That's hard to do in an unreasonable town."

"I know. I've lived here for long enough to know that only too well!"

They quieted as Sam brought out the wine and two glasses. He set them down and filled them. "Your dinners will soon be ready."

After he'd gone again, Vanessa looked at Spur and shrugged. "He's one of them."

"Great. Now all I have to do is prove it."

"And I'll do everything I can."

They sipped the wine. The front door burst open and Governor Martin Evans whisked into the room. Not pausing to look left or right he stormed into the kitchen, leaving two flapping doors in his wake.

Spur watched the doors swinging and turned to Vanessa. "I wonder what that's all about," Spur said, setting down his glass.

Vanessa licked her lips. "Sam and Martin are old friends. Sam's probably behind in his rent again."

"The governor owns this building?"

She nodded. "Half the town. And what he doesn't own, he has interest in. Governor Evans is so rich he can affort to throw around his money, and he does. He makes a lot of loans. You could almost say he's the unofficial banker of Boise. The First Bank of Evans."

"I see."

Vanessa lowered her voice. "Sam Delmonico

might have been too busy hanging innocent men and killing Mormons to think about little things like paying his rent. That'd be enough to set off Martin Evans.''

''Will you be happy if he's reelected?''

She looked into her glass. ''Oh, I don't know. But I don't have any choice, do I? At least he's a known danger. This Judd Feingold—we don't know what he's like, what he'll try to do to Idaho Territory. At least he says he supports the Mormons, which is a long way from wanting to run them out of town.'' She shook her head. ''I haven't really thought about it.''

''Yeah, you've had other things on your mind.''

''I have at that.''

Spur sipped the wine. No wonder Evans was worried about these threats. He had a lot to lose if he had to give up the title of governor.

Doors banged. Evans shot past them and walked outside. He never saw the man and woman sitting at the table, talking about him.

FEINGOLD FOR GOVERNOR, the sign in the window said.

Spur knocked on the door and walked in. The strong scent of tobacco smoke filled the air.

''Yes?'' The thin man looked up from his desk, pen in hand. His narrow eyes were heavily lidded; his chin was blue with the kind of whiskers that no razor could ever scrape off.

''You Feingold?'' Spur asked.

''That's me. The next Governor of Idaho Territory, if everything goes right.'' He smiled and rested the pen against the inkwell. Dressed in his shirtsleeves and a black vest, the dark haired man straightened up in his chair. "What can I do for you?"

Spur closed the door behind him. "I'd like to talk about the election."

"Fine! Nothing I like better than that." He rubbed his hands together. "Do you live in Boise, or somewhere else in this great territory of ours?"

"No. Just passing through."

Feingold grinned. "Then I guess you're not here to kill me."

"How's that?" Spur asked, surprised.

"I said, I figure you didn't come here to blow my brains out." Judd Feingold ran a hand through his short, curly black hair and frowned. "Maybe I should explain."

"Maybe you should." Spur took a seat.

"I've been in the county courthouse all morning—I'm a lawyer, if you didn't know. When I got back here I found this." He handed a piece of paper to Spur.

"It's rather, er, vivid account of what'll happen to me if I don't drop out of the election and move somewhere else."

The note was familiar—too familiar. Same block lettering. Different words, but Spur thought it looked to be the work of the same man. "Have you received any other letters like this? Before today, I mean?"

Feingold squinted at him and rubbed his chin. "Look, I don't even know who you are."

"Spur McCoy, United States Secret Service, from Washington, D.C."

Judd Feingold nearly fell off his chair. "Whoa! I've heard about you boys. Never figured I'd meet one!"

"You have."

"What're you doing in Boise?" Feingold rested his boots on the marble desktop.

"Investigating."

"Investigating what, may I ask?"

"Different things."

Judd Feingold smiled. "Like the vigilantes, maybe?"

"Yes."

He slapped the desk. "Hot damn! About time we got some help around here, someone who's not afraid of those holier-than-thou types!" Feingold chuckled and stared at Spur, eyes wide, face shining.

"Is this the first letter you've received?"

"Yes sir, it is."

"You've heard about the threats against the governor's life?"

Judd grimaced. "Have I heard of them? No one within a hundred miles could have missed it. Evans is playing that up for everything he can, saying that ruthless, unsavory people are trying to force him out of office, and if he isn't reelected they'll take over the whole territory. If you'll pardon my expression, Mr. McCoy, that's a load of horse shit!"

"What makes you say that?"

"Facts. As a lawyer, I deal in facts. Nothing has happened to the sitting governor. Absolutely nothing. Sure, a few notes may have been dropped off at his house, but nothing else of substance."

"And now you've received one of those notes."

"Yes."

"You think the sender's just trying to rile you both up?"

"I don't know."

Spur ran his fingernails along the right seam of his pants leg. "Any idea who might have sent it?"

Feingold grinned. "Mr. McCoy, asking me if I think the opposition's trying to scare me out of the race is like asking a married woman if she's a virgin."

"Point taken."

"If it isn't just a scare tactic from Evans, I don't have the slightest idea. Perhaps someone's having some fun. Maybe it's the vigilantes . . . ."

"You talk about them in your speechifying?"

"No way!" Feingold thundered. He stood and walked to the window. "That's one ticket to oblivion I'm not going to stand in line for. I'll admit it—I'm afraid to even mention them. I'll talk about bringing in new business, the problem of water rights, taxes, fencing the land and all that, annexation—but not the vigilantes."

"And the Mormons?"

Judd spun toward him. "Where do you stand on them?"

McCoy shrugged. "As far as I'm concerned they're entitled to live their lives wherever they want. They have rights just like the rest of us."

"Sounds like my last speech. Thoughts, ideas like that are ripping this town apart. I say we should let them in. Evans thunders on and on about how they'll destroy our chances of ever achieving statehood.''

"So this note could have been sent by someone who doesn't agree with you.''

"Yeah. Like the vigilantes.'' He shrugged. "Now that the Bancrofts are gone, maybe the last family'll move out and there won't be any more problems.'' Judd shook his head. "If Evans wins and the Mormons move back in, I don't wanna have to watch what happens.''

"I've heard a few of his speeches. Are you sure all that hatred against the Mormons isn't just campaign rhetoric?'' Spur asked.

"Maybe he is feeding on what he assumes is the commonest reaction of them. Hell, I don't know.'' He looked at the letter. "But I won't give up now. The election's only three days away. If I leave, Evans'll have things sewed up.''

"It takes guts to do that with the governor, the vigilantes, and half the town against you. That's pretty admirable of you.''

Feingold slammed a fist into his left hand. "Or powerfully stupid. Sorry, I have to kick you out. There's a debate this afternoon.''

After he left the man's office, Spur thought it over. Feingold obviously wasn't behind the letter that Evans had received. His gut feeling was that the man was innocent. A lawyer can talk a good story but McCoy sensed that he had been totally honest with him.

That led him back to the vigilantes. Suddenly, something occurred to him. He'd heard the stories that flew around the crowd watching bodies being pulled out of Bancroft's home. The latest incident had loosened up some of the populace, and whispers were passed from person to person.

Every eye-witness report of their entrance into town said that five men had ridden in that night.

Not six. Five.

Had one of them gotten cold feet? Had second thoughts? Maybe one man's conscience would not allow him to be party to killing the Bancroft family.

Or was Vanessa's comment that the sheriff was one of them true? If so, it made sense that only five vigilantes attacked the house. There were just five left.

He thought it over as he went to the Masonic Hall and waited outside for the candidates to arrive, keeping watch for a gang of kerchiefed riders.

CHAPTER TEN

"And so, fellow citizens of Boise, a vote for Evans is a vote for you!"

The packed building rattled with applause as the governor took a drink of water. Spur stood just below the speaker's platform, searching the crowd for signs of danger. He was there, he'd told himself, to protect both Evans and Feinhold.

The 200 men standing in the stuffy, hot hall quieted. The mass of humanity stretched out the door and onto the street that fronted the masonic hall.

"I'm a man of action, not empty words. Your vote will ensure that the Territory of Idaho is soon the State of Idaho, a place where we can raise our families and enjoy the riches of this great country of ours, unhindered by the seductive wiles of outsiders who'd infect us with their filthy ways!"

More applause.

Judd Feingold, sitting on the dais next to Evans, signed and shook his head.

"You don't like that, Feingold? Sorry, but they do."

Hot lead slammed into the wall behind the governor. As the explosion echoed throughout the room, the mob panicked, pushing and shoving, pressing onto each other in a mad attempt to leave. Spur bounded onto the dais between the candidates, weapon already drawn, sniffing the acrid scent of gunpowder.

"Ladies and gentlemen, please!" Evans shouted. "Calm yourselves!"

The group didn't hear his words. Spur stared down at the boiling morass of human flesh and shook his head. There'd be no way to discover who'd fired the shot.

In a few minutes it was over. McCoy stood with Evans and Feingold, looking at the boots, hats and jackets that had been dropped in haste on the floor.

"I can't believe it," Judd said.

"Didn't think I was in any danger, McCoy?" the governor asked sarcastically. "I'd say that bullet back there proves you wrong!"

Ignoring him, Spur turned to the man's opponent. "Feingold, things are getting too hot not to take threats seriously. You got any friends handy with firearms?"

He glanced quizzically at him. "Well, sure! I know a few men. Why?"

"Keep 'em with you. Wherever you go. And don't walk the streets without a pistol slapping against your thigh."

"McCoy, I can't—" Feindgold started.

"Even if you don't know how to use it, it might make some trigger-happy fool think twice. And Governor Evans, hire yourself some bodyguards." He stepped down from the dais and kicked a hat lying on the floor.

"Where the hell are you going?" Evans shouted.

"To find out who's really behind this shit!"

He walked outside. Four dozen people stood around, commiserating with each other, discussing the debate and that moment when a bullet had prematurely halted it.

But after he'd talked to 40 people he knew that no one—as usual—had seen anything.

It had all the signs of being the handiwork of the vigilantes.

"Care for more wine?"

"No, thank you. Just the check." Vanessa Gilroy opened her beaded purse.

"No, no!" Sam Delmonico said. "For you, it is on the house." He sat beside her at her table. "I—I miss you these months."

She saw the fire burning inside him. The repulsive little man took her hand. Vanessa fought off the urge to push him away. She forced herself to smile, and was astounded at the effect it had on him.

"Without you, my restaurant is dark and cold," the Italian said, his nostrils puffing. "Then you walk in and I see heaven in a green dress come down to bless me." He kissed her hand.

Widow Gilroy glanced around the room. "Isn't it about closing time?" she asked, lifting her right eyebrow.

He jumped. "I be ready in five minutes!"

As Sam Delmonico dashed off, Vanessa smiled and settled back in her chair. She was already prepared.

Ten minutes later she let Sam into her house, closed the door behind him and locked it. "Look, Sam, I won't play games. I need you. I want you!"

The Italian gasped. "That makes me so happy!" He reached for her.

The strong scent of garlic wafted over her. Vanessa took his hands. "Come to my bedroom!"

This is too easy, she thought as they climbed the stairs. Sam Delmonico was so nervous he tripped a half-dozen times before they reached the landing.

Once inside her bedroom, she closed the curtains. "Pull down your pants, Sam. I wanna see a real man!"

"Is this happening?" the immigrant said as he fumbled with his belt. Soon he unbuckled it, opened his fly and hauled down his pants and underwear.

Vanessa smirked at the tiny organ that stood there ready for her. Sam blushed under her intense gaze. It throbbed.

He ripped off the rest of his clothing.

"Onto the bed!" she said. "Now! Before I change my mind!"

"Yes—yes, Vanessa! I am dreaming this."

He took tiny steps to keep from tripping over his lowered clothing. Once there, he sat on its edge, saliva oozing from between his lips.

Vanessa quickly undressed to her chemise and

bloomers, then turned her back and went to her bureau. She extracted four lengths of black satin cloth she'd ripped into thin strips earlier that day and went to him.

"Woman of my dreams, you—you—what is this?" Sam asked in confusion.

"You know what they're for." She pushed him onto his back and hauled his skinny legs onto the mattress. Bending over him, she quickly tied his right wrist to the old iron headboard. "I will possess you, Sam Delmonico! You're mine. All mine!"

"Yes, yes," he whimpered.

Vanessa grabbed his left arm.

"Hurts!" he said. "My injury!"

"Sorry." She wrapped the satin around his wrist and tightened it. Vanessa laughed when the sudden pain went directly to his crotch.

She firmly secured his ankles to the bed's legs and stood over him, staring down at the helpless, exposed little man that she despised so much. "Do you want me?" she asked in a harsh voice.

"Yes! Please!"

Vanessa pressed her fingernails into the flesh above the knot of his left ankle and raked them upward along the hairy white flesh. Sam Delmonico shivered and pitched as she neared the point between his legs.

"You like that?"

"God, yes! Can't you see?"

Vanessa smiled and grabbed his testicles, closing her fingers around the heavy, warm sack and pulled.

"Not so hard!" he said, gasping in pain.

"Not so hard?" She yanked at the soft flesh pouch. "You killed my husband!"

Sam Delmonico howled with pain as the widowed woman's fingernails bit into his tender flesh. He struggled but the satin ropes held his wrists and ankles firmly to the bedposts. He was completely immobilized.

"Vanessa, this is not funny!" the immigrant said, bucking his hips, trying to throw off the hand that slowly tortured his crotch.

"It wasn't funny watching you and your friends string up my husband either, Sam!" she said. "At least it wasn't funny to me. But you must have enjoyed watching that innocent man die at your own hands!"

The gasping man's body reddened. "What—what do you talk of?"

"Don't try to hoodwink me, you Eye-talian murderer! I know all about it."

"You do not know what you are—"

"Sheriff MacElravie couldn't stop talking before he died." Vanessa released his testicles.

Sam Delmonico relaxed on the bed, panting, staring up at her in wide-eyed horror.

She put her face inches away from his. "Don't play dumb with me, Sam! Unless you want more of these!" She unfurled her fingers and held the sharp nails to his neck.

"No. No! I—I cannot stand that!"

"Then you better start talking." She sat on the bed beside him. "Now!"

The restaurant owner screwed up his face. "He

will kill me.''

"Who? Who'll take your miserable little life? You mean your leader? Who is that, honey?'' She touched his thigh. "Who's in charge of your gang?''

Sam twisted his face away from hers and stared at the ceiling. "Did you not hear my words? He will kill me if I talk to you!''

"Better him than me!'' Vanessa said. "You have one minute to save yourself, Sam. One minute between me and oblivion.''

Strange sounds choked from his throat. "Okay. Yes.''

"Yes what?'' she demanded.

"Yes. I am one of them. I was there when they killed your husband.'' He closed his eyes.

"There? Heck, you put the rope around his neck and cinched it up!''

"Yes.''

"I know most of the other members, I've been watching your little raiding parties in town. Last night, in fact, when I heard you, I took my shotgun outside and waited for you to pass by. Once you'd killed the Bancrofts, Sam, I took a shot at you to see if my information was right.'' She smiled and touched the bandaged wound on his arm. "It was.''

"That—that was you?'' He glared up at Widow Gilroy.

She nodded. "I'm a better shot than you are, Sam. I thank my father for the day he taught me how to handle a rifle. All those afternoons of target practice. But enough of that.'' Vanessa pressed against the blood-stained cloth. "Who leads you? Who's ultimately responsible for all these deaths?"

"Bitch!" he yelled, spitting the word at her. "I will tell you nothing. Nothing!"

"Have it your way, Sam. I gave you a chance. You just lost it." She yanked the pillow from under his head.

"Let me out now!" the immigrant said.

Vanessa smiled down at him. "I'll let you out. As soon as you're dead." She lowered the pillow.

"No. No!"

It molded to his face. The feathers trapped inside the pink cloth shifted as they pressed harder and harder against the man's nose and mouth. The Widow Gilroy sighed as Delmonico struggled, flailing his imprisoned arms so hard against their bonds that the iron bed banged against the wall.

"Darn it! Lie still and let me kill you," she said as she forced the pillow into his face. Muffled sounds from beneath it told her it wasn't working. She thought for a second, released it and squatted over his face. His gyrations hadn't yet freed his head so Vanessa sat fully on it, forcing the softly suffocating pillow into his mouth and plugging the man's nostrils.

"Bumpy ride!" she said as the pillow shook beneath her.

His body vainly whipped from side to side. She raised her knees and forced her whole weight onto Sam Delmonico's face.

As the motions below her weakened, Vanessa Gilroy remembered her husband's face, the good times they'd had—when she'd surprised him with a glass of wildflowers just after they'd moved into their new home, the first suit she'd ever sewn for him, Michael coming to her with tender lust late at night after bolting out on some emergency call.

She thought of the babies that hadn't been born, the long days that would have stretched out into years with her husband, the plans they'd had to tour the capital cities of Europe when he had closed his dental practice.

Vanessa sniffed and realized that the pillow was still. She shook her head, slipped her legs to the side of the bed and stood on the floor. Gingerly, the widow lifted the pillow from Sam Delmonico's head.

The tortured expression on his face told her all that she needed to know. The terror and suffering he must have endured before he'd gasped his last breath didn't begin to pay back the horror she'd lived with these past few weeks, Vanessa thought, but it helped.

"You'll never kill another innocent man," she said, and went to her bureau.

Back at the bed with a knife, she bit its blade through the satin and laughed as his left arm flopped down, lifeless and slowly growing cold.

"I don't buy that, Evans!" Judd Feingold stabbed the air with his finger.

"Your spending habits are no concern of mine, Feingold," the governor joked.

"You paid someone to take a wild shot at you during the debate this afternoon!" He stabbed the air with his finger.

"Why?"

"I can say it in two words: sympathy vote."

The governor folded his hands and laid them on the oak desk. "Your imagination is matched only by your stupidity, Feingold."

The candidate advanced on him. "Yes. I've been so stupid, believing you'd run a clean campaign like the decent, honest man you say you are!"

Evans tapped his fingers on the desk. "Haven't you wised up by now? You should know how it is. There's no place in politics for an honest man."

Judd Feingold groaned. "That kind of thinking's what's wrong with this territory! It's men like you who're gonna run Idaho into the ground!"

"Give it up. Drop out now, Feingold. Get your ass outta town."

Silent, the man reached into his pocket and retrieved a folded piece of paper. "I got your note!" he yelled and threw it onto the desk."

"I don't send letters to assholes." Evans kept his hands folded and didn't even glance at the square of paper.

"Who'd you get to send it for you? Huh? One of your friends, the vigilantes?"

"I don't know what you're talking about and I don't care. Out!" Evans roared, rising to his feet.

Feingold smiled. "Tell your friend—the one who sent me the letter—that I won't back down now. I'll fight you all the way to the polls! I've got right on my side!"

"Aren't you forgetting something, Feingold?" Evans said. "Your support of those ungodly, perverted, heathen Mormons?" He said the word like a curse. "They're against every principle the United States of America was founded on. They go against our laws and the will of God. And I'll do everything in my power to keep men like you from ever holding office!"

Judd Feingold shook his head. "You double-talking bastard. You'd even kill me to win."

"Keep out of my way." Evans leaned across his desk. "Just keep out of my way! I don't wanna see your ugly face until after the election." He curled his upper lip. "After I win, I just might invite you to my celebration here at the mansion."

"If I ever do run into you again on the street I'll stand upwind." Feingold walked to the door. "I can't stand your smell!"

Evans smiled as his opponent walked out of the room. He picked up the letter that lay on his desk, unfolded it, read it and walked to the fireplace.

Might as well get a little blaze going, he thought, and threw the paper onto the grate.

She fastened the last button and looked at herself in the mirror. The dress suited her, Vanessa Gilroy thought. She wasn't in mourning any more. She was through with feeling sorry for herself.

As she glanced down at the reflection of her shoes she saw the body lying behind her on the floor. Not long until it was time to get rid of him.

But she couldn't put off the hardest part of her task. The sturdy woman grabbed Sam's ankles and pulled him out of her bedroom. Reaching the stairs, she walked down them backwards, carefully fitting her feet on each descending step, watching as the dead man's head flopped up and down, banging into the wood. The effect was comical.

She hauled him to the front door and walked into the kitchen. Eyeing the barrel beside the pie-safe, Vanessa pumped spring water into the kettle and lit the stove. A good cup of tea would calm her down, she thought. As the water simmered over the yellow flames lapping up from the fire box, the widowed woman pushed the barrel into the entryway.

She'd never put a man inside a barrel before, but she set her mind to the task, stuffing the naked body inside the cask, rearranging stiffening arms and legs until she'd fully succeeded. That done, she hammered the lid onto the barrel with three nails until it was completely shut.

The whistle from the kitchen distracted her. She poured the water into a teapot and added a heaping spoonful of tea, replacing the top before the odor-laden steam could rise up to her nose.

Vanessa sat at the kitchen table and wrote a short note, detailing Sam Delmonico's crimes, stating that he'd been a member of the vigilantes and had been brought to justice—just like Sheriff MacElravie had been.

She copied the note, word-for-word, and stuffed the duplicate inside the barrel just in case the second one blew off. With another nail she fastened the first note to the lid and stood back, pleased at what she'd done.

After enjoying her cup of tea, Vanessa Gilroy rolled the heavy barrel out front and pulled her carriage beside it. Straining her muscles, the woman managed to finally heave it into the carriage. The vehicle creaked under the weight. She pulled the black scarf over her face and rode to the sheriff's office.

She halted the horse and looked around. The town was deserted. Besides, who'd notice if someone saw a barrel being dropped off a carriage? It could be a delivery or something.

The sheriff's office was dark. She pushed both feet against the barrel. It lurched forward and banged down onto the dirt. The dust softened the blow; the barrel landed intact.

Smiling, Vanessa drove back home, enjoying the cool evening air and the new freedom that surged through her.

It really was too bad though, she thought. He did cook a good steak.

CHAPTER ELEVEN

Spur McCoy yawned, rubbed the ache in his lower back and wondered why he couldn't get to sleep. It must be well past midnight, but something kept him awake.

Too many unanswered questions, he told himself, staring at the darkened ceiling. Too many bodies. Not enough suspects. And the election was just a few days away.

Hmmm. He rolled up to a sitting position and pushed his feet into his boots. Maybe a short walk would clear his head and let him get some rest.

He pulled on his coat and walked outside of the Goldrush Hotel. Everyone in town seemed to be asleep but him. He rambled down the boardwalks fronting the various businesses, wandering aimlessly, trying hard not to think about anything at all. Just breathe deep and smell the night, he told himself.

It worked for a while. He walked two blocks and was weary enough to return to bed. But he figured he might as well finish the third block before heading back.

He dragged himself down the street, his boots shuffling in the dirt, looking straight ahead. Something didn't seem right. Something was lying in the street.

McCoy peered through the darkness at the black lump as he approached it. It looked out of place, to say the least. Adrenaline coursed through his veins. He quickened his steps. What was it?

Spur sighed. Just a barrel, he thought, and kicked it. To his surprise, it didn't move. Both lids were firmly secured, he discovered while examining it. What in hell was inside?

He squatted and succeeded in rolling it a foot or so. It moved crazily as if a heavy object was inside. Strange, the Secret Service agent thought, as he sat on his heels and rested.

Then a lighter colored patch on the barrel's surface caught his eyes. Spur felt it. It was smooth, cold from the night air. And it moved.

It was too dark to tell, but Spur knew what it was. Must be a label of some kind. He tore the paper from its fastener. It easily came off. Rising, he stared at it.

The darker shadings that covered it seemed to indicate writing, but he couldn't be sure. Frustrated, Spur fumbled in his pockets and found one single match. He lit it on the bottom of his boot and held the flaring stick up toward the paper. The words roused him to full consciousness.

VIGILANTES BEWARE!

> Sam Delmonico is no longer with you.
> He's gone to his reward—in hell!!! I've
> sent him there like I did his fellow
> vigilante, Sheriff MacElravie. This judge
> and jury found Delmonico guilty of
> murder and executed him this night.
>   Don't try to find me . . .

The match flared up and flickered out, plunging
the note into darkness. Spur had seen enough.

Sheriff MacElravie a vigilante? And the Italian
restaurant owner, too? Who had found out? And
who was killing them?

He glanced at the darkened sheriff's office. They
wouldn't have a new sheriff until after the
election. Who could he talk to? Spur set his jaw.
He had no choice.

He ran toward Thistledown Avenue. The houses
and trees flew by him. It was a hard, fast run but
Spur was in shape. He was only slightly out of
breath as he opened the great iron gate and sped
up to the front door.

Lights shone in the downstairs windows.
Someone was up in the governor's mansion. He
banged the knocker three times and waited,
huffing.

"What in hell—Spur!"

He groaned. "Hello, Lacey."

"I knew you'd come back!" She pushed his chest
and stepped outside. "My father's here with

company, but we can go out to the garden again and—"

"No. I'm sorry, Lacey. I have to see your father."

"Why?" The young woman frowned. "Don't you like me anymore?"

"Of course I do. This is business. There's been a murder and I've found the body."

"A murder!" She blew out her breath. "I must say, you do come up with the best excuses." She backed inside the door. "He's in the library."

"Thanks, Lacey." He kissed her forehead and went there.

"I don't know, John. I don't know if I want to take the risk," Governor Evans said.

"Sorry to interrupt you!"

The two men, startled, turned and stared at Spur as he walked into the library.

"No, no, Mr. McCoy," Evans said with an obviously forced smile. "What brings you here at this hour?"

Spur glanced at the man who stood next to Martin Evans. Thin, bearded and white-haired, he was dressed in an expensive suit.

The governor laughed. "John Shepherd, my lawyer. You can trust him."

"Alright. Since you're the highest elected public official around here I thought you should know. There's been another murder."

The two men looked at each other.

"The vigilantes?" Evans asked.

Spur shook his head. "At least, I don't think so." He turned for the door. "I can't wait to explain.

Bring a hammer and come with me!''

"A hammer? Okay, McCoy. Just let me grab my coat!''

He headed out to the entryway. Lacey stood there in a flowered blue robe, huddled against the chill air blowing through the still opened door. "I figured you wouldn't be staying long so I didn't close it.''

"Thanks. See you soon!'' Spur yelled.

"Hold on, McCoy! What's all this about?''

"I don't know, governor. I found a barrel sitting in front of the sheriff's office. A note was attached to it. I figured you better be there when that barrel got opened.''

"Okay, that sounds fair. But how does murder fit into this?''

"We'll find out.''

Four minutes later they stood assembled around the ordinary wooden cask. Shepherd held a match to the note, and Evans read over his shoulder, his lips moving with each word.

"I don't believe it!'' Evans said. "It's not true! Sam Delmonico was a fine man. He wasn't the type to ride around at night burning down houses and hanging people! For God's sake, he was a family man!''

"His wife up and took the kids to Augusta,'' Shepherd pointed out. "That must've been two years ago, and she hasn't been back since. He's changed since then.''

Evans stared at his lawyer.

"You got that hammer?'' Spur asked.

"Sure.'' Evans handed it to him.

"We'll know for sure in a minute or two." Spur rammed the tines under the lid and pried. The nails resisted the pressure for a few seconds, then loudly squeezed out from the wood. "Progress," he said, and grunted as he pulled the hammer sharply toward him.

He repositioned it and yanked as hard as he could. The lid was an inch from the barrel. In a new position, Spur finally succeeded in popping it off. He bent down. "Can't see a damn thing. Got another match, Shepherd?"

"What? Ah, sure!" He handed one to Spur.

Evans and Shepherd crouched down behind him. He struck the lucifer. Yellow light exploded and danced from its tip, illuminating the contents of the barrel.

Spur shook his head.

"I'll be damned!" the governor shouted. "It is him!"

"That's Sam Delmonico alright, though I never saw him like that."

The man's naked body lay crammed into the barrel. His head lolled at an unnatural angle. Sightless eyes stared up at the three men.

"You ever hear any talk about him riding with the vigilantes?" Spur asked.

"No. Nothing. You, John?"

The bearded man shook his head. "Uh-uh. That man was clean as a whistle."

"Someone sure thought he was one of them."

"Damn! This has to stop!" Evans said.

Spur stared at the dead man. "Seems like an anti-vigilante group has sprung up."

The lawyer moved closer to the barrel. "But how'd he die? I don't see any rope burns on his neck, stab wounds or slashes."

Spur rose and stretched his calves. "Assuming there aren't any on the parts we can't see, I'd say there's only one way he could have been killed."

"Poison?" Governor Evans asked.

"Strangulation."

"I don't know who'd do something like that to old Sam. He was the best cook in town," Shepherd said, lighting a third match from the dying flame.

"What happens now, Evans?" Spur asked.

"What do you mean?"

"I mean, there's no sheriff. You're in charge. What do you want to do?"

He set his jaw. "Find the bastard who killed Sam. What the hell do you think?"

"Use your head, Evans!" Spur's voice was so sharp that the big man turned to him. "We can't leave a man's bare-ass body here in the street for the women to see in the morning. I know you have an undertaker in this town. With all the work he's had lately, I don't think he'd mind one more job. Go wake him up. Me and Shepherd'll bring the body."

"I'm not used to taking orders—"

"Just do it!"

Evans frowned, looked at the dead man again and threw up his hands. He walked away without a word.

"You know where the undertaker's place is?" Spur asked the lawyer.

"Huh? Sure, yeah."

"Something wrong, lawyer?"

"No. It's just—I don't know. It makes you wonder if anyone in this town's really safe."

"I know what you mean. Help me get him out of there. We've got work to do!"

Between the two of them they managed to extricate the cold, stiff body from the barrel. The lawyer gritted his teeth during the task, seeming to force himself through it. Spur was surprised at John Shepherd's obvious revulsion at touching the dead man.

"You're not running for sheriff, are you?" Spur asked.

"No!"

McCoy nodded. "Good!"

It was dawn by the time he left the undertaker. The sunlight seared his eyes. Moaning from lack of sleep, Spur rubbed his face, lowered the brim of his hat and walked down the boardwalk.

"McCoy! I just heard!"

The voice was familiar. He looked at the figure racing up to him.

"One of the vigilantes was killed and you found the body. Right?"

"That's about it, Feingold."

"Whoa, boy!" He hopped from foot to foot, practically dancing a jig. "Anything else?"

He forced himself to speak through his exhaustion. "Judging by your reaction, Judd, I'd say there's a lot more. The killer left a note with Delmonico's body. In it, he said that Sheriff MacElravie was a vigilante, too. Doesn't that news brighten your day?"

Judd reared back. "Don't misunderstand me, McCoy. I don't think murder's right, and I certainly don't approve of what happened to these men. But I'm glad they're gone. If those two were vigilantes that means there's only four of them left. Their ranks are dwindling, my friend." He looked up at the sky. "I just wonder who's doing it?" He sucked his cheek.

"You and me both, Feingold. You and me both!"

Too weak, Vanessa thought as she sipped the tea. Was it too much water or too little tea? She sighed and put down her cup. She wouldn't worry about it. Nothing could worry her today.

She hadn't woken until ten that morning, but then it had been a long night. The widowed woman, still dressed in her underclothes, went to her bedroom and flung open the old walnut dresser. What should she wear today? Yellow? She smiled. Yes.

Yellow was a great color for an execution.

CHAPTER TWELVE

What the hell did she want with him?

John Shepherd clutched his books as he walked to Vanessa Gilroy's house. He'd been greatly surprised when she showed up at his office that afternoon, asking that he stop by just after supper to go over some of her late husband's papers.

Shepherd had readily agreed. He could always use some extra money—even from her—and it would get him out of Martin Evans's way for a while. That man was starting to get on his nerves, the lawyer thought. And she certainly wasn't too hard on the eyes—or other parts of his body.

He thought it was rather odd that she'd waited all this time. What was it, two weeks since her husband's death to settle things like that. But he figured she'd spent all her time mourning.

John Shepherd grimaced when he thought of the

lie he'd concocted for Governor Evans, saying he'd had to attend to a dying woman on the south side of town. She hadn't made out a will and he couldn't possibly get out of it. Evans didn't like sharing Shepherd with anyone else, but when he'd informed the governor that the woman would probably deed much of her estate to the city, and that she'd voted for him, the big man had given his permission.

A figure slowly approaching him made Shepherd readjust his shirt tails and straighten the position of his hat.

"Afternoon, Mr. Shepherd," Lacey Evans said.

"Good afternoon to you, Lacey." He turned and watched the young woman walk away, frowning. If only she wasn't the governor's daughter. And if only he wasn't on his payroll.

He put those thoughts out of his mind. That's dangerous territory, he told himself. Don't go exploring where you know you'll be in trouble.

He turned down Mapleview and quickened his steps. Dusk was deepening into evening; the last light faded from the western horizon, blotting out the church spire that had been outlined against it.

It was night.

He rapped on the door at 313 Mapleview and waited. Nothing. Was she hard of hearing? Frustrated, he knocked twice as hard and kicked the door for good measure. It slowly swung inward.

"Hello? Mrs. Gilroy!" he yelled.

Silence. The slice of the house's exterior he could see didn't contain the woman, so he pushed it fully open.

"Come on in, Mr. Shepherd!"

He turned and blanched at the unbelievable sight. "Widow Gilroy!"

"Thank you for coming. We have a lot of work to do together this evening," she said.

Confusion boiled in his mind. "But—but—"

"But what?"

Shepherd dug his fingers into the hard leather bindings of his legal books, pressing them to his stomach. "Mrs. Gilroy, you're naked!"

"I'm what?" She looked down at her body and smiled. "Why, so I am! I must have plumb forgot to put on any clothes!" She ran her hands through her perfectly curled red hair and approached the middle-aged man. "How silly of me!"

"I—I—" He stared at her. "What are you doing? Keep away from me!"

"Now, Mr. Shepherd, you aren't afraid I'll bite you, are you?" She grinned wickedly as she advanced toward him. "A big man like you?" She glanced at his crotch.

He pressed his back against the door, closing it. "Mrs. Gilroy! Your behaviour is scandalous!"

"What's wrong, John?" She placed her hands on her thighs and rubbed them up and down, miming kisses.

"Have you no shame?" he asked, confusion and sexual heat swirling in his mind. She was naked and beautiful, but he couldn't touch the woman. He couldn't bear the thought. It was too sickening after what had happened.

"No!" he shouted, shrinking from her. She was almost within arm's reach.

"No what?" She moved her head in a tiny circle,

staring at him from lowered eyelashes, moistening her lips.

"Widow Gilroy, I'm a god-fearing, Christian man! Stay away from me!"

"God-fearing? Hell, John! What's a little sin between friends?" She throatily laughed.

"Stop. Please!" He panted.

Vanessa nodded and stepped back. "Okay, okay. I just figured that we could—never mind. That's not the reason I asked you here anyway." She walked to the rolltop desk in the corner of her parlor.

Shepherd relaxed. He'd almost allowed himself to lose control. "What—what was it?"

"I need some legal advice. Mr. Shepherd, what should I do? I found out the lawyer I'd engaged to conduct my husband's business is crooked."

"What do you mean, crooked?" He looked down at her round, pink buttocks as she bent over at the desk.

"Unethical." Vanessa turned to face him. "He's a thief. A criminal. A murderer!" She put her fists on her hips and arched her back, lifting her breasts.

John Shepherd smiled. His natural inclination for legal work overcame his unease. "I was wondering why you'd suddenly asked to see me. Look, I'd be happy to counsel you, Widow Gilroy, but do you think you could put something on? That's rather, ah, distracting."

"Of course! How silly of me. I haven't been thinking right for weeks now." She walked to a chair which was draped with a pink robe.

"I guess that must be why you're dressed like that."

"You mean *not* dressed." She twirled her obscenely exposed body like a girl showing off a new dress, laughed and slipped on the robe. "Is this alright?" she asked, tying it around her body.

He took one last look. "Ah no, Mrs. Gilroy. Your—your chests are still out."

Vanessa looked down. "Oops!" She smiled and pushed them under the cloth.

She was a strange woman. If she'd been any other female in Boise he would have jumped her. But not her. Not Widow Gilroy. Just his luck!

"Fine. I need your help in trying to figure out what to do to this man. I have to find a way to trick him into admitting everything he's done."

"I see." The thought of being instrumental in bringing one of his colleagues to his knees enthused him. "What can I do for you?"

"Well, start by putting down your books. On that table there!" she brightly said.

He did so. "And now?"

"Turn around. Just turn around for a minute or two. Let me work things out. I know I'll have to surprise him from behind."

"Okay." As he stood there, facing the far wall, Shepherd regretted his revulsion toward her. It could have been fun. If only—

He felt her breath against his right ear.

"Pretend to be him. Pretend to be Gus Procter!"

"Sure!" So that was the name of her double-dealing lawyer! Wait until I tell Evans, Shepherd thought. He never did trust the big city lawyer.

A hand fastened around his stomach. A second plastered to his neck. Gentle pressure at both spots told him he wasn't supposed to move.

"Is this a good hold?" she asked, huffing.

"Yes. You'd have to do it tighter, though." His body felt warm and good against hers. Was she trying to trick him into pleasuring her?

"Like this?"

Her grip crushed him, digging into his belly. Vanessa Gilroy gripped his chin and yanked back his head.

"Hey!" he yelled.

"John Shepherd, shouldn't a lawyer who's killed an innocent man deserve the worst punishment?"

"Of course. Let me go, Vanessa!" Confusion washed through his mind.

"And shouldn't that man be punished without waiting for a trial?"

"Yes. Yes, of course!" The arm constricted his neck. This wasn't any fun at all. Pain stabbed into his body. "Vanessa, what're you doing to me?"

"What I should have done a long time ago, murderer!"

She was serious! John struggled against her, but the woman was surprisingly strong. His unused, underdeveloped muscles were weak.

"I don't know what you're—"

"Yes you do!"

Tight. Tighter. He couldn't move his arms. She crushed him, digging into his neck, throwing him off balance.

"Do you confess to your crimes, John Shepherd?" she hissed.

"What crimes?"

"Don't play strupid with me! You were there. You're one of them! You killed my husband!"

"I don't know what—" The agony spread through his body.

"You shouldn't have made me watch!" she screamed. "I recognized you and your horse the night you came with murdering thoughts in your mind!"

Her arm bit into his throat for a blinding second, then eased off. "Alright. I was there!" he gasped. "Let me go, Vanessa!"

"You killed him! You all killed him! And now you're going to get your reward!"

He gagged under the choking weight. John Shepherd lurched forward, desperately trying to extricate himself from the woman. But she held on, moving with him, squeezing his neck harder and harder until she cut off his air supply.

The ascetic lawyer gasped. The ceiling shimmered in his mist-filled eyes. He made one last effort to break free from her clutches as the pressure at his throat increased. His lungs seemed to explode. Sweet lethargy poured through him. The room dissolved as every muscle in his body went limp.

An odor penetrated the darkness of his brain. A harsh, poisonous odor that was somewhat noisy. A loud smell?

The thought was enough to rouse him. John Shepherd opened his eyes. The odor was strong, sickening, dangerous. He saw Vanessa Gilroy, fully dressed, splashing some liquid around the room.

Vanessa! Where was he?

He tried to sit up but couldn't—something was holding him down. "What—"

"Save your voice for the Almighty, John!" she said, walking to him. "You'll be talking to Him real soon!" The widow smiled as she worked.

Shepherd gyrated on the couch before realizing he was firmly tied to it.

Vanessa walked up to him, held the tin can over his body and tipped it, spilling its contents onto his body.

One drop landed in his eye, stinging it. The scent seemed familiar. Then he knew.

Kerosene.

"No, Vanessa! Don't do this!"

"I'm only following your advice," she said. "Taking the law into my own hands. Punishing a known murderer!" She threw down the can. "Besides, it was good enough for the Mormons!"

"I'll do anything—anything!" John pleaded.

This wasn't happening, he thought. This wasn't supposed to happen. He'd promised them!

"You've already done enough!"

The bound man lifted his arching head to look around the room. Everything was splattered and soaked with kerosene. He flopped back down when the pain in his throat threatened to make him black out again.

"No!"

She put a handled basket under her arm and tied her bonnet firmly onto her head. "Sorry, I have to be going now. I won't see you again"

''Please!'' The terror sickened him but he gave into it, firmly believing what was occurring. This wasn't a dream. This was cold, hard reality.

Vanessa Gilroy reached into the basket and took out a lucifer match. ''Goodbye, Mr. Shepherd.''

She struck the match and threw it onto his stomach. It flared up, igniting the liquid, turning his shirt front into an inferno.

The widow laughed, struck two more matches, threw them into the room and quickly walked out.

Adrenaline speeding his efforts, tortured pictures of that night when they'd hung Michael Gilroy whirling in his mind, John Shepherd arched his neck and tried to blow out the flames.

High. Higher. The curtain of fire spread along his shirt, burning through it, charring his chest hairs and searing his skin.

The pain was too much. The screaming man closed his eyes as the blaze engulfed him.

CHAPTER THIRTEEN

I should go see her, Spur thought, picking his teeth after his supper. Maybe the good Widow Gilroy knew more than she was telling him.

As he walked out of the Goldrush Hotel, men with buckets ran past, yelling at each other. Young boys screamed as they raced after their fathers. Water?

Fire! Then he smelled the smoke, grabbed the fire bucket that hung beside the door outside the hotel and followed the contingent.

He saw the flames before turning down Mapleview. Orange-red light slashed the inky sky, boiling and billowing in its destructive fury. Ash fell to the street like dry snow. A shiny horse-drawn firewagon pulled up as he joined the bucket brigade.

It was Vanessa Gilroy's house.

The small quantities of water they hurled at the flames evaporated before they had the chance to do anything. The fire flared up. Flames shot out the lower windows of the old house, forcing the men back with blasts of heat.

Spur shook his head as he watched it burn, standing amidst gasping men and women whose faces glowed redly in the darkness.

It was hopeless, but he helped pass the buckets that were filled from the big metal tank that had been hauled there. Was she there? Was she safe, or already burned to a crisp?

"Anyone inside?" he asked the squat man in line beside him.

"Hell if I know. It just seemed to go up like tinder. No one could go in and check."

The fire fed on the dry wood. The men stood back as the top floor crashed in on itself and the flames rose higher into the black sky.

The house on Mapleview turned night into day. Bizarre, dancing shafts of light bathed the citizens of Boise as they watched the rushing flames bathe it, slowly eating away at the structure, reducing it to worthless rubble.

Spur set down his bucket, took off his hat and wiped the sweat that had formed on his forehead. Had this been the work of the vigilantes, too?

If so, why would they hurt Vanessa Gilroy?

Governor Evans strolled up and recognized Spur in the eerie light. "What in hell's going on here, McCoy?"

"I don't know. Maybe the citizen's committee again." He shook his head. "I just hope Vanessa wasn't inside."

"That is her house! Or it was, anyway. But it couldn't have been them, McCoy. They haven't touched a woman in all their doings."

"What about the Bancroft place?"

The governor frowned.

"They killed Jake Bancroft and two of his wives."

Evans shrugged. "Not directly. Besides—"

Spur touched the man's shoulder. "Look, governor. I don't wanna hear any more of your reactionary rhetoric concerning the Mormons. Save it for your speeches."

The husky man frowned at him.

"No. No!" a woman screamed.

Vanessa Gilroy walked up beside Spur, her steps shaky, staring up at the blaze. She held a cloth-covered basket under one arm and clamped a hand over her mouth as she watched the carnage unfurl itself with increasing fury.

"Vanessa! Thank God you're alive. I didn't know if you were inside or what." Spur touched her shoulders.

"My house. Everything I own. It's just—just—" Her hair glowed with the inferno's orange light.

"At least you're safe."

She dropped the basket and took two faltering steps toward the blaze. The middle-aged woman shook her head, open mouthed.

The people standing around, drinking in the spectacle, slowly moved away from the woman, respecting her grief.

"Maybe you shouldn't watch." Spur took her

hands in his. "Don't you want to go somewhere else? Anywhere else but here. It won't help to look."

She violently turned to him. "No, Mr. McCoy. I have to watch!"

"Okay."

Her face shone in the red light. "I was just taking some food to a woman I know who's sick on the other side of town. I wasn't gone more than an hour."

Her voice was so weak and strained that Spur had to bend his ear to her mouth to hear her over the crackles and snaps issuing from the blazing building.

"I was just doing a good deed—and now look what those vigilantes have done! They've ruined me!"

Governor Evans walked up. "McCoy, I've been asking around and no one saw the vigilantes ride through here earlier this evening."

Spur gripped the woman's hands. "That's nothing new, is it, Evans? No one ever sees them. There's too much fear in this town, not enough guts!"

Vanessa Gilroy laid her head against Spur's chest. He gathered her in his arms and held the woman.

The fire seemed to die down momentarily. Then a tremendous explosion rocked the house, hurling the last remnants of window glass out all four sides. The building buckled and the lower walls crumpled into black splinters laced with darting red tongues.

"Salamanders," Vanessa said, still watching.

"What?"

"My husband used to say that salamanders played in the fireplace when we sat before it on cold winter nights. Little red lizards that bathed on the coals, enjoying the warmth, nourishing themselves on the fire."

She was going out of her mind. "Come on, Vanessa. Let's get you somewhere."

The woman pulled away from him. "No! I don't want to. I'll stay until the end!" Widow Gilroy walked closer to the blaze, clasping her hands before her.

A grizzled old timer walked up beside Spur.

"Nasty fire," he observed.

"That it is. You see who started it?"

"Mister, I live right across the street. I was home all night, and I didn't hear or see the vigilantes ride through here. I've always seen them before. Not tonight."

Spur grinned. "You've seen them?"

"Sure!" He rubbed his bald head. "I'm too old to get involved in the games all these other folks are playing. I've seen them two or three times. It's always been the six same horses, the same kerchiefs over the men's faces."

"Can you remember anything about their mounts? Something that might help a man find out who they are?"

The man smiled at Spur. "Why?" he asked sharply.

"It's time someone did something about the vigilantes. Don't you agree?"

"Hell, yes!" He stuck a finger into his right ear and twisted it back and forth with so much force that it seemed he was searching for something buried inside it.

"Well?" Spur asked.

"Well what? Oh, them horses. One of their beasts stands out. I've seen it clear two times. A big horse, black as a moonless night. Its coat shimmers. About 17 hands high, maybe." He pulled out his finger and looked at it. "White blaze on its forehead."

"Great. Have you ever seen this horse in town? Tied up to a hitching post, or with an unmasked man riding it? Any idea of who it belongs to?"

"I don't know. Don't get out of my house much. I just sit in my rocker and watch what goes on through the winders. The missus gets out more, but she's got no sense about horses—or much of anything else any more, the poor dear."

"You've been a great help, mister—"

"Steel. Johann Steel."

"Thanks, Mr. Steel."

"Yeah, well, a man's got to do something to keep him from going crazy." He wandered off, the excitement forgotten, back to his own home.

The blaze had nearly consumed its fuel. Jagged timbers jutting erratically into the air framed heaps of broken wood and charred furniture.

A paunchy man dressed in long johns with a coat thrown over his shoulders shouted for attention. "Okay, men! Let's put out the hot spots! Make sure it don't spread nowhere else!"

The bucket brigade started again. The ten or so

men had things well in hand, so Spur turned back
to Vanessa Gilroy. The woman stood silhouetted
against the dying flames, surveying the
destruction.

He went to her. "You have a place you can
stay?"

"Yes," she said, her chin firm. "I'll stay with
the Widow Parkin. Millie's lonely since her
husband passed on and wants company. She said
I could if I ever sold the house." Vanessa laughed.
"Too late for that now."

"Look, Mrs. Gilroy, I'm sorry."

"Don't—don't say it. Please."

"Fine. You know where I am if you need me."

"I surely do. Goodbye, Mr. McCoy."

Spur nodded at the somber expression on her
face. She walked away, leaving the basket she'd
dropped lying in the dirt as a gust of wind covered
it with fine, white ash.

"Shepherd! Shepherd!" Martin Evans walked
through the crowd, searching for his lawyer.

Where the hell had that man gone, he wondered.
First he says he has to take care of some old lady's
will, and now he's disappeared.

Just like him to duck out in a time of crisis. The
governor went to Shepherd's house; it was dark.
A quick search inside turned up nothing.

His horse stood sleeping in the rickety shelter
behind the lawyer's house. It hadn't been ridden
lately.

Evans shrugged and returned to his mansion,
enjoying the walk. As he stretched his legs he

remembered the burning house and Spur McCoy's questions about the vigilantes.

Who the hell had done that to Vanessa Gilroy?

Millie Parkin had been more than kind, taking Vanessa in without question. She'd counted on the old woman and hadn't been disappointed.

Now as she pulled the lavender-scented sheet up to her chin, trying to get comfortable in the strange bed, Vanessa wondered if she'd done the right thing.

Not the execution—John Shepherd had deserved to die. That was obvious. But burning down her own house? All those memories of her late husband?

She shook her head on the goosedown pillow. The past was just that—passed. And she still had momentos—his knife, gold pocket watch and billfold that she'd placed in the bank after his murder. That, and the small diamond ring on her finger, were enough.

Besides, the fire should stir up the citizens of Boise into action against the vigilantes. She had to work slower than she wanted in removing those evils from this earth. Maybe the public outcry over their latest crime would make them think twice befor striking again, before they ended any more innocent lives.

Then she could execute the others, one by one, until none were left. The thought comforted her and she turned on her side and tried to sleep.

Of course, there was still one man that she hadn't identified. One man who always sat on his horse when the others did the dirty work. The tall man who always rode a different horse and disguised his voice during every crime.

Their leader, Vanessa thought, biting her lower lip. Who was it? Would she ever find out? And if not, would she ever be able to blot out the memories of his raucous laughter as he forced her to watch her husband's murder?

Three men met in a valley outside Boise. Masked, they dismounted, secured their horses to a clump of saplings and squatted, talking in low voices.

"Where's Shepherd?" one asked.

"I don't know."

"Men, we can't afford to take any chances," the tallest said. "MacElravie and Delmonico are dead. People are starting to talk about this, and now someone's burned down Widow Gilroy's place and made it look like we did it. We're losing our grip on this town!"

"What the hell can we do about that?" a shorter man asked. "Hell, we don't know who's killing our own! It could be anyone at all!"

"Gentlemen. Gentlemen. Do I have to remind you of what'll happen to the rest of us if we don't discover the man who's decimating our ranks? You won't be doing any complaining with a knife buried in your back! So work on it. Spend every second trying to solve this little problem."

"And what'll you do?" the vigilante challenged their leader.

"Everything I can on my end. Now ride back into town!"

CHAPTER FOURTEEN

Goldrush Street was hot and dusty. A carriage rattled by, thickening the air with a brown haze that spurted up in its tracks.

McCoy was checking horses. A big black stallion with a white blaze on his forehead, the man had told him. If a vigilante had indeed ridden that horse it had to be in town. He couldn't know if the man was a reliable source of information. But then again, he didn't have anything else to go on.

So he searched the town, discreetly looking at every horse that walked or trotted by, or that stood drinking from the wooden troughs.

He saw dozens of them. Hipshot, whinneying beasts of every color and description were lined up before the businesses and homes of Boise, Idaho Territory. Bowed-backed nags barely able to keep on their feet; roans, sorrels and bays; the odd stallion or two looking for love; placid geldings simply waiting for the return of their owners and another long, hard ride through the countryside.

Some of the horses regarded him curiously as he passed, raising their heads, licking water from their mouths, flaring their huge nostrils. Brown eyes warily regarded the man.

After he'd traveled the length of Goldrush on both sides, Spur walked down the other streets. A few horses were tied up at the hitching post but no big black beasts with slashes of white on their heads.

Undaunted, he stopped by the two livery stables in town, posing as a potential customer, and checked out the merchandise. Nothing. The horse might as well not exist.

The man who lived on Mapleview could have been mistaken, or could have passed on false information. Or, Spur reasoned, the owner of this particular horse was being careful. Extremely careful.

Dusk deepened into the blackness of night.

Vanessa Gilroy straightened her bonnet and knocked at the back door of the huge brick building. It finally opened.

"Hello, Clem," she said sweetly as she walked into the bank.

"Hello yourself, Widow Gilroy. You're looking pretty this evening." The thickly-haired, short man sighed and locked the door. "Been a long day, it has. So you really came to get it? You're really going to do it?"

Vanessa patted the banker's shoulder. "Mr. Jackson, you don't have anything to worry about. I won't withdraw every cent my husband deposited in your bank. Just some of it—to help out with unexpected expenses. After all, I lost everything in that fire." She smoothed a mask of despair onto her face.

"You poor dear," Jackson said, shaking his head. "I understand. As long as you won't break the bank, I can help you out."

"Thank you!" She looked around the empty building and shivered. Only two lamps had been turned up in the vault. "It's cold in here. Do you think we could just do it?"

"Of course. Come this way."

"I won't feel safe until I'm back at Millie Parkin's place," she said, following the waddling middleaged man. "That's why I had you let me in the rear door after regular hours, don't you know. I don't trust the streets any more. Why, if someone saw me coming in here after hours they'd assume I was withdrawing a large amount of cash money. Heaven knows what would happen if one of the vigilantes found out about it!"

Clem Jackson turned to look at her, his big doe eyes softening in the thin light. "I don't think you have to worry about that, Vanessa. They don't rob folks. Leastwise, they haven't yet."

"Just their lives."

The banker grunted, held an oil lamp in his left hand, stooped over, cracked his fingers and twisted the dial on the face of the vault door. "I forgot and already locked the dang thing up."

"What's the matter, Clem? You in a hurry to leave work or something?"

"No, no. It's just that I could—"

"I know. I could use a drink myself!"

Jackson beamed. "Now that's being honest. Nothing I like more than an honest woman!"

She heard a click.

"Okay, you can come in now."

The banker swung open the door. She stepped up to the circular aperature and was amazed at the thickness of the walls.

The vault was the size of a small room, lined with metal shelves stuffed with numbered leather sacks. Each sack was simply tied shut—not locked.

"How'd you ever get such a big safe?" Vanessa asked.

"It's a vault, and they dragged it here during gold-rush times. Boise needed one this big because of all the money that flowed through her during those days." He looked around. "It's seen lots of riches in its day. More than you or I ever will." He walked inside, carrying the lamp with him.

Vanessa sniffed. "Where's my husband's deposit?"

"Oh, ah, right here."

Clem Jackson rummaged around for a second and turned to her, smiling. "Here it is. Deposit number 6-0-5."

"Thank you. Could—could you bring two chairs? This might take a few moments." She gripped the heavy bag.

"We could move outside—"

"No. No! I feel safer in here."

"Fine and dandy." Clem handed her the oil lamp. "Be right back."

Alone in the vault, Vanessa opened the bag and extracted $3,000. That was surely enough, she thought, as she stuffed the hundred dollar bills into her purse. For now. She retired the bag.

"Here we go." Clem pushed two chairs inside.

They sat facing each other. Vanessa pretended to open the bag for the first time and gaped at the amount of gold, silver and bills it contained. The thirty year-old woman glanced up at the banker. "This calls for a celebration of sorts. Doesn't it?"

He peered at her. "Celebration? What you getting at, Vanessa?"

She revealed the small bottle of whiskey she'd put in her purse before coming. "A drink or two?"

He licked his lower lip. "I never say no to a lady, Mrs. Gilroy."

The banker was practically salivating. Vanessa handed him the bottle. "You first!"

Clem straightened his back, removed the cork and took a healthy swallow. He closed his eyes as the numbing liquid slid down his throat and entered his stomach. "Ah! Fine stuff you brought there."

"Just the best money can buy," she said sweetly. "I figure if we're going to drink it might as well be good stuff."

He proffered the bottle to her, wiping a stray drop from his lower lip.

"No, you go again. I have work to do!"

Fifteen minutes later, Vanessa had three piles of bills on her knees. The bottle was nearly empty as Clem shakily set it on the vault floor.

"You—ah—heh, heh. You about done there, Vaneshy?" The man couldn't seem to keep his feet firmly on the floor. They kept slipping forward, threatening to spill him from the chair.

"Just about. I'm doing some figures in my head."

He was drunk, she thought. Almost time.

"Well, how about a drink?" She held the whiskey out to him.

He raised a coarse hand to his face. "Oh, no. Oh, no!"

Widow Gilroy stuffed all the money back into the bag.

"Something wrong, Clem?" she asked him.

"My God, it finally happened, just like my ma used to tell me when I was a squealing brat!" He patted his cheeks.

"Clem, what's the matter?"

The banker turned to her with sad eyes. "I done drunk so much my nose fell off!"

She deliciously laughed. "I told you—only the finest for you. That's why I didn't have any. Just a drop of that liquor makes me—well, you don't want to hear about it." She had cleared her lap and retied the string that kept the bag closed.

"It shore do the trick." He coughed and looked around the vault. "You know, sometimes I wish all thish was mine. It'd be sho easy to forget that it ain't, to clean it all out and go live somewhere else."

"Now Clem, you'd never do something like that." The widowed woman rose and replaced the bag on the second shelf. "Crimes have a way of coming back to haunt you."

"Ah heck, Vaneshy," Clem said, slapping his knee. "Not if you're careful! If no one knows you did it there's no danger."

"But if someone finds out?"

He fastened a red-eyed gaze at her. "Ah. Well, I guess it would be obvioush—me 'n the money disappearin' at the same time."

"Yes. Folks always know who did something like that. Bank robbery. Cattle rustling." She stood before him. "Murder."

"Well, yeah. Guess I'll leave it here." He looked up at her. "You about finished?"

"Yes, Clem." She picked up the bottle. "And so's this whiskey. You realize how much you drank?"

He screwed up his red face. "I'm sorry. Sometimes when I start I can't stop."

"That's alright, Clem." She released her fingers; the bottle crashed onto the metal floor.

Jackson looked around, startled, holding his ears as the sound echoed and reverberated in the small metal room.

"Oh! Look what I've gone and done!" Vanessa said.

"I don't mind, girlie. It'll clean."

The woman slipped behind him. "Here, let me help you out of that chair." She grabbed his shoulders. As the squat man rose, Vanessa Gilroy pushed him back so hard that he stumbled and toppled over.

"Hey! Take it easy! I'm not a well man!" he said

on his knees.

"I know why you've been drinking so much. It's your conscience. You can't live with yourself since you started riding with the vigilantes. Can you?"

Clem Jackson placed his palms against the floor and tried to rise from it. "Now hold on there, Vaneshy!"

"I know all about it."

"Stop talking nonsense," he said to the wall, unable to turn to face her.

"Nonsense? Why, Sheriff MacElravie, Sam Delmonico and John Shepherd all said you were one of their own before they died," she lied. "Besides, I recognized the horse you rode on your nightly raids. Not your brown gelding, but the one you keep out on your son's spread. The big black stallion with the white blaze on his forehead!"

He twisted over on the floor and landed on his buttocks. "You—you know what? What'd they tell you?"

She smiled. "Everything."

Vanessa Gilroy bent and picked up the remaining upper half of the bottle. "Everything except two small details. Who's the fifth man? And who led you into doing this, Clem, huh? Who told you to go out with him and kill my innocent husband in cold blood? Who was it?"

The banker dissolved into tears. "It—it sounded like a good idea at the time. I didn't wanna do it. But he—he—he talked me into it."

"Who? Who was it? Who's your leader?"

"No. I can't tell you." His shoulders slumped forward. "I can't tell you or anyone."

"Are you so sure about that, Clem?" Vanessa waved the deadly glass weapon in the air between them. "If you don't tell me right now I'll send you to the same place I sent George, Sam and John!"

The sobbing man gazed at her with bloodshot eyes. "You killed them?"

She laughed. "Of course. Haven't you been listening to me? I'll kill you, too, if you don't start talking. Now, Clem!"

He crawled back to the wall and leaned against it. "Vaneshy," he said, blubbering. "I just can't. Now you get outa my bank!"

"No. I've got work to do." She pretended to lunge at him.

Clem Jackson struggled to his feet and grabbed the woman's arm. "No! Don't do it!"

She wrenched free from his alcohol-soft fingers and stepped back. "Who else rides with you?"

"Alright. Alright!" He tore at his hair, standing on shaky feet. "Rex Cutshaw."

She laughed. "The saddle maker? I don't believe it. I don't believe that leather stitcher's the man in charge of the vigilantes!"

"He ain't. Cutshaw's his second. If you don't believe me, go ashk him! But I can't tell you anything elsh!"

"I'll ask him. Right after I take care of you!" Vanessa Gilroy advanced on the trembling, tear-stained man. "Don't worry about it, Clem. Maybe they have banks in hell!"

She slammed the broken glass onto his scalp with such force that it drove the man to the floor. Bright blood sprang from the wound as Clem

Jackson fell face-first. The sound of his impact—flesh slapping against steel, the tinkling of coins in his pocket—echoed in the vault.

Vanessa threw down the bottle. It smashed beside his face. "Clem?" she called.

Nothing.

"Clem?" Louder this time.

Had that done it? Panting from her exertions, Vanessa squatted next to the downed banker. She smiled at the needles of glass that peppered his right cheek, making it look for all the world like a pincushion. She shook his shoulders but he continued to lie still.

Vanessa touched his neck. The pulse was there, but weakening. He was unconscious.

Good. She walked to the vault's door and looked back inside one last time. He lay there surrounded by spilled whiskey and broken glass—and two chairs.

She breathed deeply and hauled them out, replacing them behind the first two desks that obviously needed them. No sense in taking any chances, in having any questions asked.

Vanessa Gilroy pulled the door shut but didn't spin the tumblers. It was Friday night. No one should go into the bank until Monday morning.

By then Clem Jackson would be dead from loss of blood or lack of air. As she straightened her clothing and walked to the bank's rear door, Vanessa remembered the first time he'd shown her the huge vault and told her how it was airtight. Anyone who stayed in it for more than an hour or so would die of asphyxiation, he'd said.

When his employees arrived on Monday morning, they'd find him and assume he'd gone into the vault to drink after work and swallowed down so much that he'd passed out and accidentally died.

Just what she wanted, Vanessa thought. She walked into the darkness outside the bank and calmly closed the door behind her. The last thing she needed was the remaining vigilantes to be too wary.

Especially a leather stitcher named Rex Cutshaw.

CHAPTER FIFTEEN

Spur spent a frustrating weekend. Between meetings with Governor Evans and Judd Feingold, he had questioned the people of Boise about the vigilantes but ran up against the same wall of silence that had hounded him since he'd arrived in town.

On Sunday afternoon, he'd provided security during the governor's final speech, held in the middle of town. It went smoothly. No problems.

And no further threatening letters were sent to either candidate. Judd Feingold apparently hadn't been scared off by the one he'd received, for he energetically waged his campaign of peace and co-existence, paying boys to plaster the whole town with posters and hiring white-haired women to spread the word, trying up until the last moment to change the voters' minds.

McCoy checked every horse in town, but the black stallion with a white blaze still eluded him. It wasn't in Boise, for he'd looked virtually everywhere—even poking his head into the small stables behind houses.

When he began questioning people about it he got even more discouraged. No one save for the man who lived across from Vanessa Gilroy's old place would admit to seeing it. Just the very mention of the beast made decent men and women uncomfortable.

Spur had napped Saturday night and walked the streets until about three A.M., on the alert for another vigilante raid. But all was quiet. He repeated the same schedule Sunday but once again, the power-hungry killers didn't disturb the town.

McCoy had figured things would heat up but they seemed to be simmering. What was going on?

On Monday morning, he sighed and glanced at his haggard face in the cracked mirror. Men who were named as vigilantes were dropping like cows in a waterless desert. If they didn't recruit more members soon they might as well disband entirely. Whoever was killing them was doing a bang-up job.

He shrugged at his reflection and unbuttoned his shirt, then used its tails to mop his forehead. This early in the morning, before nine o'clock, it was already hot in his hotel room. It was hot all over Boise.

It was election day.

Later that morning, Spur visited two saloons to

listen in on the local gossip. Clem Jackson, a banker, had been found dead in the vault. A broken bottle and a sticky stain on the floor seemed to indicate he'd gotten drunk, accidentally closed the door and suffocated to death.

Suffocated, Spur had thought, sitting in the saloon, listening to the young buck's words. Why did that seem so familiar?

And was this death accidental, or had this Jackson been killed? Was he mixed up with the vigilantes?

After leaving the saloon he spent the rest of the afternoon watching the polls. People were orderly, and it seemed every man in Boise lined up to make his mark on the town's political history. The governor's shills worked the line, urging the men to vote for Evans. Those that said that they had, received two dollars.

The shouted praises of the governor's record— and Judd Feingold's pained expression as he came to vote an hour before the polls closed—seemed to point out the inevitable.

Two hours later, a nervous young man stood up at the podium in the Masonic Hall. It was official—Martin Evans had been re-elected, but by a surprisingly narrow margin—269-231. Evans made a point of publicly shaking Feingold's hand and slapping him on the back, but his glee spilled out in his words and the quick movements of his squat body.

"McCoy," Evans said to him after the results were announced. "I'm having a victory celebration tonight at the mansion. Fifty or so of my closest friends will be there. Why not stop by and have a drink? Now that I'm out of danger and you're out of a job."

"I'll try," he said, smiling at the man, "but I might be busy."

Something about Evans rubbed him the wrong way. It always had, but he couldn't determine what it was.

"Then I'll be looking for you!"

Spur walked over to the losing candidate. "You gave it your best, Feingold. I guess bigotry and hatred ruled the day."

The thin man shook his head. "That's the way it goes. Excuse me, I think there's a bottle of whiskey somewhere with my name on it." The man pushed through the crowd away from Spur.

McCoy blew out his breath and returned to his hotel room. He should eat, but he wasn't hungry. He could go to the mansion but he didn't feel like celebrating. Thoughts about the vigilantes and their killer boiled up in his brain. He worked out so many possible explanations that he finally had to put the subject out of his mind.

Spur answered the insistent knock on his door. "Vanessa!" he said in surprise.

"I had to come see you." She pushed past him and paced back and forth in his room. The woman removed her bonnet. Red hair flashed back and forth.

"How have you been since the fire?"

"As well as can be expected. Millie's been such a dear, putting up with me these past few days." The widowed woman touched her left cheek. "I'm afraid I've been a terrible burden on her."

"I'm sure she enjoys your company. Well, it's election day. Did you hear who won?"

Vanessa halted at the window. "Evans?"

"Yeah."

"It doesn't matter to me. Nothing matters."

"What can I help you with?" Spur closed the door and went to her.

"You heard about Clem Jackson?"

"Was he the banker that they found dead in his vault this morning?"

She nodded. "Well, I have it from a reliable source that he didn't just drink too much and pass out. He was killed because he was one of the vigilantes."

It figured.

"Who told you this?" he asked, touching her shoulders.

"That doesn't matter. What does matter is the other piece of news I've received." She took a deep breath. "I need you to come with me on a visit to a man I think is one of the last two remaining vigilantes." Her gaze burned into him.

"Wait a minute. Slow down!" Spur said, shaking his head. "Who is this?"

She frowned at him. "Rex Cutshaw. You probably don't know him. He makes saddles here in town. Spur, if you don't go with me, I'll go alone!"

"And do what?" he asked her.

Vanessa bitterly laughed. "You can't imagine how it's been, knowing that some of the men who killed my husband are alive and walking the streets while Michael rots in the churchyard!'' She broke from his grip and stepped back. ''If there's anything I can do to bring them to justice I'll do it—even if it means going there by myself.'' She strode to the door.

''Now wait a minute, Vanessa!''

She paused, her hand at the knob.

Spur thought for a moment. ''Okay. I'll go with you.''

''Fine!''

Five minutes later they were walking along a tree-shaded street. The sun hadn't quite set, but deep shadows cut into the ground.

''What are you planning on doing?'' Spur asked. He figured it was best to be with her to ensure that things didn't get out of hand.

''Among other things, find out if it's true. Most important, I want the name of the other vigilante. Their leader. If Rex Cutshaw is one of them, I'll rely on you to force him to tell me—us.''

''Maybe you shouldn't be there.'' He tugged on her arm to slow her quickening pace.

''Don't try to stop me, Spur!'' she said. ''I want to know the truth! I want to hear him admit he's one of them! Besides, you wouldn't even know about him if I hadn't told you. You owe me this one.''

He sighed. ''Okay. How far is this place?''

''Right up the street.''

Vanessa gripped her purse and hurried toward it, with Spur struggling to catch up with the determined woman.

They neared a small, ramshackle house on the outskirts of town. As they walked up to it and opened the rickety, paint-peeling fence, a man stepped out of the building.

"You Rex Cutshaw?" Spur asked.

"That's me." He nodded to Vanessa. "I'm just going to vote."

"Too late. The polls closed hours ago. Evans won."

The stocky man grinned. "Oh, well. Guess he didn't need my vote nohow."

"We have to talk." Spur walked toward the man and stood inches from him, waiting.

"Okay," Cutshaw said, his neck popping. "Come on inside the place."

"I thought you'd never ask, Mr. Cutshaw."

His house smelled of tobacco and old bacon. Spur watched Vanessa's nostrils flare at the unappetizing odor as they were seated in Cutshaw's parlor.

"Can I get you something to drink?" he asked, his face expressionless.

"A whiskey would suit me just fine!" Vanessa said. "And one for Mr. McCoy."

"Let me handle this," he whispered to the woman after Cutshaw walked out of the room.

"Fine. We'll do it your way." She crossed her ankles and primly placed her hands on her knees.

The saddlemaker returned with two small glasses filled with amber colored liquid. "Darn!" the man said, smiling to reveal two cracked front teeth. "I forgot all about your drink, Mrs. Gilroy. I'll be right back." He set down the glasses on a small table and disappeared once again.

"I can't wait," Vanessa said. She walked over to the table.

"My, you're thirsty."

"Be quiet!" After a few seconds she returned to her rail-backed chair.

Rex walked past the table and handed the third glass to Spur, who took it and sipped the bitter liquid. "I see you've already started," he said, smiling broadly as he went for his whiskey. The complicated business over, he eased into a chair, and took a swallow. "What can I do for you? Need a special, customized, deluxe saddle or something?"

"No," Vanessa said.

Spur cut her a look. "Mr. Cutshaw, I'm in town inquiring about the dangerous situation here."

The man looked into his glass. "Kinda bitter." He raised his eyebrows and downed its contents. "What dangerous situation?"

"All the murders. The threatening letters that were sent to Governor Evans a few days back. The criminal activities that have occurred here without so much as one citizen standing up to the men doing them."

Rex burped and licked his lips. "Why come to me about all this? Mr. McCoy, is it? Mr. McCoy, I know leather and I know horses inside and out. I can make you a saddle that'll last you a lifetime. But this talk about—about—"

Spur glanced at Vanessa, who smiled at him. "Mr. Cutshaw? Are you feeling ill?"

The man set down his glass and yawned. "No. Guess I worked too hard today. Can't seem to hold up my darned eyelids."

"We'll be out of here soon, Rex," Vanessa said.

The middleaged man slumped in his chair. "Whoa! Boy, I am tired. Must be the whiskey . . ." He grabbed the curved wooden arms and held on for a second. His entire body went limp and slid to the floor.

"What in hell?" Spur asked, walking to him.

"Just something I put in his drink, Spur. Nothing to worry about!" Vanessa Gilroy smiled at him.

Spur grabbed the woman's arm. "Vanessa, I told you. I'm in charge here. I didn't tell you to slip a sleeping power in Cutshaw's drink!"

"It won't last long. I gave him enough to put him out, but only for a few minutes." She looked down at the unconscious man. "Rex always was a lazy sort."

"Vanessa, give me your solemn word that you won't interfere again. If you're right about this man he's a dangerous criminal, far too dangerous for you to be toying with him!"

"You're right. Doesn't he looking positively lethal right now, laying there passed out on the floor?" The red-haired woman laughed.

"You know what I mean," he said, irritated at the woman's boldness. He'd lost control and hadn't even been aware of it. "Just sit still and keep your mouth shut!"

The woman returned to her chair. "Yes, daddy." A wry smile played on her face.

Spur bent over Rex Cutshaw. "Wake up,

godddamnit!" he shouted. "I have some questions
I needed answered!"

"He is drugged, after all. Give him fifteen
minutes."

"Okay, fine." He didn't turn back to her. "I need
some rope," McCoy said, unbuckling the man's
gunbelt. "Might as well tie him up while he's
helpless."

Vanessa clapped her hands together like a child.
"What a clever idea, Spur McCoy!"

"Did you think of it?"

"Why else would I have knocked him out?" She
gasped. "I'm not as dumb as you appear to think
I am."

"Let's not—" Spur shook his head. "I'll be
back."

He went into the kitchen. Piles of dirty tin plates
and stained coffee mugs spilled over from the table
onto the floor. Greasy rags and a half pound of
odorous green bacon sat on the stove, surrounded
with flies. Spur breathed through his mouth as he
rummaged through the mess. No rope.

Frustrated and wary that Rex Cutshaw would
wake up while he wasn't there, Spur dashed out
the back door and saw a hank of hemp hanging
from a hook by the door. He grabbed it and ran
back into the parlor.

Vanessa looked up at him. "Don't worry. I
haven't killed him yet." She smiled brightly.

"Nice that you can keep your sense of humor
at a time like this," Spur said.

He rolled the man onto his stomach and quickly
bound his wrists, securing the knots tight enough

so that the coarse rope bit into his skin. That finished, he picked him up and dumped him into the chair.

"Would you have thought to do this?" he asked the woman as he tied the man's ankles to the chair legs.

"Don't underestimate me, Mr. McCoy!" She tapped her feet on the floor. "It's been just about long enough. Get some water and—"

He shot her a harsh, penetrating glance.

"I'm sorry." Vanessa's eyes were steely. "I'll do as you told me. I won't interfere."

Spur shook his head as he went to the kitchen. He found a salt-glazed jar filled with water and walked back into the parlor with it.

"Okay, Cutshaw, time to wake up!" He tilted the clay vessel over the man's face. A few drops spilled onto his cheek. When there was no sign of consciousness Spur upended it, sending a quart of water splashing down.

Cutshaw coughed, spluttering against the sudden rain, rapidly blinking. His shoulders surged back and forth in the chair.

"What—what—" he blubbered.

"Hello again, Cutshaw!" Spur said viciously.

"What—who tied up my hands?" He shook his head, flinging crystalline drops of water flying through the air. "What in hell's going on here?"

"This is a questioning, Mr. Cutshaw. You're going to answer my questions about your vigilante activities here in Boise. Now!"

"I don't know what the hell you're talking about," the man protested. He blew out liquidy breath. "You've got the wrong man, mister, and I'm damned mad about it!"

"I don't think so. And don't use that kind of talk in front of a lady!"

"Lady?" He looked around the room in confusion until he saw Vanessa. "Oh, yes, Mrs. Gilroy. You're still here."

"Rex—"

"Now then, Mr. Cutshaw," Spur said, cutting off the woman's words. "How long have you been riding with the vigilantes?"

"I already told you, you have the wrong man! Who in hell's been bad-talking my good name?"

McCoy glanced at Vanessa. "Someone in the know. Someone who knew the truth."

"Clem Jackson!" she blurted.

Rex stared at the widowed woman. "What?"

"Clem Jackson told a friend of mine who told me!"

"But old Jackson's dead."

"He wasn't last Friday afternoon when he pleasured Millie Parkin!" She gazed at him triumphantly. "Everyone knows a man can't keep a secret when he's—"

"That's enough, Vanessa!"

"—he's putting his thing—"

McCoy lunged at her. "Shut your mouth, woman!"

Vanessa stepped back and lowered her head.

"Cutshaw, I'm a federal law enforcement officer. I have the power to arrest and to kill if necessary. You don't want that to happen, do you?"

The saddlemaker struggled against his bonds. "Why? I didn't do anything! Let me out!"

Spur sighed and drew his Colt. "All Uncle Sam cares about is a body, a name to fit a crime. I guess yours is as good as any other man's."

"Now hold on!" Cutshaw drew in breath so rapidly that he hollowed his cheeks and whistled. "Maybe I do know something about all this."

"Uh huh."

He looked down at the floor. "Suppose I was one of them vigilantes. What'll happen to me?"

"That depends," Spur said, casually pushing the muzzle of his revolver to the man's throat.

Cutshaw inched back until his hair was plastering against the cushion. "On what?"

On how much help you are to me."

Cutshaw's wide eyes stared from Spur's hand, traveled up his arm and finally stopped at his face. "Okay. Alright! I'm tired of it anyway! It's gotten out of hand."

"What's gotten out of hand?"

"The—" He bit his lip.

"The killings? The murdering of innocent men and women? The fires? The rampages?" He bent toward the man. "The taste of blood gets sickening after a while, doesn't it? It isn't as much fun. You don't feel the rush!"

"Yes." Rex Cutshaw squeezed his eyes shut and gently shook his head. "I couldn't leave. They wouldn't let me stop, said I was in it as much as they were and if I didn't ride with them to burn down the Bancroft house they'd kill me." He opened his eyes. "Shoot me dead! There wasn't nothing I could do. I had to go. Don't you understand? I had to!''

Spur grimaced. ''You never should have started. Oh, the little lady has a question for you. Don't you, Vanessa?''

He heard the woman's boots clicking on the floor behind him. ''Yes. Who's your leader?'' she asked as she stood beside McCoy. ''Who tells you what to do? Who was it that forced you into killing those women?''

''It'll look good in court.'' Spur eased his Colt away from the man's neck and stepped back. ''Soften up the judge's heart. Make him lenient.''

''I don't know if I can tell you that.'' Cutshaw seemed incredibly interested in Widow Gilroy's boots. ''My life wouldn't be worth living.''

''Come on, now, Rex,'' the woman said. ''You don't want me to kill you, do you?''

Vanessa gripped a full sized .44 revolver in both hands. Her arms were strong and steady. This was a woman used to handling firearms.

''Damnit!'' McCoy yelled.

''Spur, back off. If you try to rush me I'll shoot him! I mean it! He killed my husband. It's only right that I make him pay his debt to me!''

The fury in her voice proved her point. ''Okay, okay Vanessa. We'll do it your way.''

''Now, Rex, who is it?'' Her voice was controlled, low. ''Who threatened you if you didn't keep riding with him. Hmmmm?''

Cutshaw whistled a little tune and looked at the ceiling, acting as if she didn't exist.

She lowered her aim toward his crotch.

Rex laughed. "Get off it, girlie! You ain't gonna use that thing."

"Maybe I won't kill you, but I'll be happy to ruin your future dealings with women!"

He looked at her aim and blanched. "You wouldn't!"

Vanessa smiled. "Are you willing to bet your thing on that?" She jabbed the barrel into his fat crotch, making the saddlemaker howl with pain.

"Trust me, she can do anything she puts her mind to." Spur stood back and watched the scene unfold.

Cutshaw pursed his lips. "Alright, alright, girlie! Just pull that weapon outta my crotch!"

"Not until you tell me who it is!"

Spur smiled as the man glanced at him. "Sorry. I can't control her. You're on your own."

"It's—it's—"

"Yes?" She forced the revolver harder against his genitals. "Yes, Rex?"

He sighed. "Hell, it's the most powerful man in town. The one who owns half the buildings, who built the Masonic Hall, who's got every politician wrapped around his little finger." Cutshaw took a breath and shook his head.

"You mean?" Vanessa asked.

Rex nodded. "Yes. It's him. Governor Evans."

CHAPTER SIXTEEN

"You just lost yourself a ball, Rex!"

"No, wait Vanessa!" Spur warily walked to her. "It all fits. What man in town would benefit most from the vigilantes? Who constantly needs to deal with enemies? And who's been screaming about the Mormons ever since I got here?"

Vanessa bit her lower lip, thought, and finally removed her revolver from Rex Cutshaw's groin. "Martin Evans. Governor Martin Evans! It has to be true!"

"It is!" The saddlemaker gritted his teeth. "The man's gone crazy. No one can control him!"

Vanessa turned to McCoy. "What do we do now?"

"Well, they must have elected a new sheriff today." Spur gently took the weapon from the woman's hand. "Maybe me and Mr. Cutshaw here should visit him."

"Yeah. Just get me away from that woman!" He shrank back in the chair and tried to force his knees together.

A half hour later, after delivering the man to a surprised greenhorn sheriff by the name of Tabor, Spur and Vanessa walked down Goldrush Street in the early evening air, arm in arm.

"Know why I brought you along?"

"Hmmm? Ah, no. Why did you?"

"I didn't trust myself. I thought I might kill him before he had the chance to tell me. Just like all the others."

He stopped. "What?"

"You know how it is, Spur. A woman's got to do what she thinks is best. When they made me watch my husband's murder I studied them. Memorized every detail I could—their horses, their clothes, their heights, even the kinds of kerchiefs they wore over their faces. I was right about George MacElravie, Sam Delmonico, John Shepherd and Clem Jackson, but I didn't have a clue who the other two were." She turned to him. "Clem was nice enough to tell me about Rex, though he wouldn't name Governor Evans."

Dark thoughts burned in his mind. "Vanessa, you didn't—"

"So I figured I only had one more chance to discover the truth. I brought you along for insurance."

He studied her face, but it was concealed by deep shadows. "Did you kill those men?"

"Of course!"

"All four of them?"

"Yes, Spur," she said impatiently. "Haven't you been listening to me? I had to bring them to justice. They destroyed my life. You understand, don't you? I had no choice—not with a dishonest sheriff!"

"I'm not sure. It's a big shock."

"Why Spur McCoy, you said yourself not an hour ago that I was capable of doing anything I put my mind to." She patted his arm. "Can we be going now? I can't wait to get back to Millie's and take a rest. These boots are killing me!"

Spur smiled at the comment and escorted her to the house. He'd worry about what to do with the woman later—after he visited the mansion.

Every lamp in the huge building must have been lit for the windows shined so brightly that a glow surrounded the mansion. As Spur walked up to the house the sounds of laughter and music issued from inside.

So Evans was celebrating. Why not? He'd won the election. He'd forced nearly every Mormon out of town. He was in complete control of everyone but the sheriff, McCoy thought. It was time to correct that.

The front door was wide open. Spur walked in. The hall was empty save for coat-covered chairs and that ancient domestic who'd given him a rude greeting the last time he'd seen her.

"Take your jacket?" the wrinkled woman asked.

"No, thanks."

She huffed. "Suit yourself. They're in the ballroom—down the hall to the right."

He nodded to her.

The noise grew louder as he moved along the panelled walkway, passing oil paintings of men who he assumed were the governor's antecedents. What would they think of him now?

The hall led into a huge, open-beamed room. Four musicians played something that seemed vaguely French on a small stage. Elegantly dressed men and women danced before it while others milled around the tables stocked with liquor and platters of food. Spur smiled in greeting to a few vaguely familiar faces and moved through the crowd.

Despite the opened windows the ballroom was hot, steaming with the sweat of the toadies gathered around their leader, eager to snatch a crumb from his overflowing plate. The men drank. The women laughed and flirted. But everyone seemed slightly uneasy, as if they expected the roof to cave in. Even the bright lamp light shimmering from the crystal chandeliers lining the walls couldn't sweep away the darkness within the people assembled there.

Evans wasn't in sight. He asked a few people if they had seen the Governor but they simply shrugged and moved away from him. McCoy walked past the rows of glasses and bottles of gin, whiskey and Scotch and out through the floor to ceiling double doors. He entered a garden. The same garden where he and Lacey had so much fun.

Where was Evans?

"Stop the music!" a voice boomed out.

Spur instantly returned to the ballroom. Martin Evans stood on the podium in front of disgruntled musicians who put down their instruments.

"Ladies and gentlemen, I propose a toast." The governor raised a glass. "To another four years of peace and prosperity for the people of Boise!"

Men yelled and stamped their feet. Liquor sloshed down throats. And above them all, looking down on his flock, Governor Evans drained his glass and threw it onto the floor.

The resulting crash cheered the celebrants. "Dance! Drink! Eat!" he said, gesturing in the air. "Tomorrow we go back to work!"

Another round of laughter. The two violinists, the cellist and the flautist started playing again, taking up where they'd left off. Spur sank back into a corner and waited.

Lacey breezed into the room dressed in a gown worthy of her name—an incredible concoction of lace and white silk that cast a veil of purity over her luscious body. Evans embraced his daughter, kissed her on the cheek and grabbed a glass out of a passing man's hand. He laughed and bolted down the contents.

Spur moved out of the line of sight. If Lacey saw him it could complicate things. He certainly couldn't touch the governor in front of fifty people—a veritible private army. No. He'd wait to make his move.

A mature woman, jewels dripping from her neck, asked Spur if he'd seen her blue and white brocaded purse. He smiled and shook his head.

"So what the hell good are you to me?" she said

in a heavy European accent.

He sighed and bided his time.

Fifteen minutes later, after two more visits from the drunken foreigner, he watched Evans slap two men on their shoulders and walk laterally across the ballroom, jokingly pushing aside the couples who whirled there.

Where was he going? Spur slowly moved toward him and quickened his pace as the governor disappeared into the garden. He hurried after the man.

Martin Evans stood facing a rose bush. Spur heard the soft trickle of liquid splashing onto its leaves.

"That isn't very elegant, Governor Evans. Pissing on flowers."

Surprised, Evans turned on him, recognized the face and turned away from him. "No. But I nearly flooded my pants in there, and that wouldn't be the best way to start a new term in office." He went about his business. "You, ah—decided to join my celebration after all?"

"No. I came here to talk to you about Rex Cutshaw. He's just confessed that he's a vigilante."

Evan's right hand shook up and down. "So?" he asked and faced Spur, buttoning up his black trousers.

"So he and you are the only vigilantes left. He said you led them. You planned the raids and ran them. Very efficiently, I might add."

Evans smiled and stepped toward him, searching his face in the dim light. "Thanks, McCoy. Coming from a man like you that's a real compliment. If that's all, I have to rejoin my guests."

"I've got some more news for you, Evans. I know who's been killing your friends—the sheriff, your lawyer, all of them."

The governor stopped before him. "Yeah? Well who is it?" His voice was harsh.

"Not me. Someone you'd never suspect." Spur worked out his words with care. "Someone who's damned mad at you, who's still walking the streets, waiting for the right time to send you into the next world."

Evans brushed a wet spot on his fly. "You trying to scare me, McCoy? Hell, my men can find anyone."

"Not this time. You don't have so many men left, do you, Governor? Four of the best of them are dead."

"Get to the point! What do you want? Money?" He laughed. "No."

Evans peered at him and frowned. "Get your butt off my property, McCoy! I don't take kindly to smart-mouthed double-talkers!"

"You're forgetting something, aren't you?"

"I'm trying to forget you."

"You're under arrest!"

"Shit. Boris, now!" he yelled.

Spur ducked a second before lead cleaved the air over his head. He rolled across the bare earth and slammed into the jasmine bush as screams and rustling feet echoed inside the ballroom. There, looking out through the tangled leaves, he drew his revolver and waited.

Evans had darted out of sight. The gunman who'd fired at him hadn't shown himself. Spur cursed. The man did indeed have protection who followed him everywhere he went. Even when he took a—

"There's no way out, McCoy!" Evans shouted. "You made a big mistake coming here and expecting me to let you drag me off to jail!"

Spur fired at the sound of the voice. One bullet.

"Good try, but not good enough!"

"Evans, the sheriff knows all about this," he lied. "If I'm not back there in ten minutes, he'll come looking for you!"

Gunfire exploded in the garden. The bush shook around him as bullets raced through it, dislodging a shower of white petalled flowers.

"Bullshit! Ralph Tabor's a friend of mine! Hell, I put that man into office!"

This wasn't getting him anywhere. Spur surveyed the land behind him. Three feet of dense yew trees fronted a brick wall.

McCoy used every trick he knew, silently moving through the dense tangle of trees, crouching, carefully pressing his feet one at a time to the ground. Then gunfire broke out over his head.

The explosions reverberated in the walled garden, zipping past him again and again until the silence consumed them. The smell of gunpowder burned his nose and the air was blue with it.

He looked out among the twisted trunks. The garden was about 30 feet square with plenty of shadows and bushes. Lots of hiding places.

"Father, what's going on?"

The voice electrified him. Spur turned to see Lacey standing in the doorway, lit up from behind 'ike an angel atop a Christmas tree.

"Father, is Spur McCoy out there?" Lacey yelled
into the garden from the ballroom doors.

"Get back in the house!" Evans shouted. "Do
you want to get yourself killed? The man's gone
crazy! He's liable to plug you full of bullets!"

"No, daddy! You're out of your head!"

Spur finally got a firm position on the man.
Evans must be behind the plaster garden bench
that sat near the doors.

"Move!" the governor screamed.

"No!"

"Thomas, take her to her room and come right
back!"

"Ah, yes sir!"

A man darted from the trees on the far side of
the garden. Spur peeled off a shot. The lead
slammed into the man's right hand.

Lacey screamed.

"Son of a bitch!" The gunman fired madly into
the yew trees as he ran for the ballroom, grabbed
the young woman and pulled her out of sight.

"You're endangering my daughter, McCoy!"
Evans said, taking a shot.

It sailed harmlessly into the air. "No way.
You've been doing it ever since you thought you
were the law in Boise."

"I am the law!"

Now, Spur thought. The time was right. He
hunched over and moved through the trees,
gliding silently through the thin trunks on either
side. Three seconds later he stood beside the
bench.

"Don't move, Evans!"

The man stared up into Spur's barrel. McCoy

smashed his boot into the governor's right hand, sending his weapon flying away. "It's over."

"No. Damnit, no! I'm not gonna let a little man, a little, sniveling man like you take me down!" Evans said. He got to his feet. "No one tells me what to do!"

Spur backhanded the governor's chin. The stocky man reeled, cursing and rubbing the bruised skin.

"Bastard!" he spat.

"They say you see yourself in other men. I guess they were right. Let's go!"

CHAPTER SEVENTEEN

The next morning, Spur wired General Halleck the news and stopped by the sheriff's office. He jingled the big key ring as he walked in. Rex Cutshaw and Martin Evans glared up at him from their respective cells.

"If you don't have any food, I don't wanna see your ugly face," Cutshaw said.

"Sorry, fresh out of green bacon." His voice was bright.

Evans rose from his cot. "I'll see you hang for this, McCoy!"

"Save your breath. Did you hear, ex-governor? Judd Feingold's being sworn in this morning. They're putting together an emergency ceremony to make it all legal. Some of your friends won't be here to see it. They're packing up and leaving town. Just like Sheriff Tabor did last night."

"Damn you!"

Spur laughed. "But don't think I'd leave you here all day without someone to look after you."

The front door opened.

"That must be him now."

"McCoy? Where the hell are you?"

"Back here!"

A tall, clean-shaven man walked into the rear room. "That them?"

"Yup. Keep your eyes on those two. I don't trust either of them—especially the short, fat one." He pointed at Evans.

"Will do." The man smiled. "Sure was surprised to run into you on the street this morning."

"Same here, Forester."

"I wasn't planning on staying in town but you had to go and remind me."

"Right. Libertyville. Three years ago. I saved your ass, marshall!"

"A U.S. Marshal?" Cutshaw said. "Hear that, Evans? He's a marshall!"

Spur sighed. "I'll be back for them tomorrow morning to escort them. But I've still got some loose ends to tie up." He tossed the keys to the man.

Forester grabbed them and winced. "Sure. No problem. I didn't want to spend a week with my sister anyhow. My brains'd fall out if I had seven days of peace and quiet."

McCoy laughed as he walked out.

"You can't see her," Lacey Evans said as they lay panting in her bedroom.

"Why not? Are you jealous?"

"Of course!" She smiled. "But that's not the reason. Vanessa Gilroy stopped in here to say goodbye to me. She left town."

He sat upright. "When?"

"First thing this morning." Lacey arched her back and stretched. "She left on the eight o'clock stage. I guess she didn't like it here in Boise, and I don't blame her." Her voice was breathy; her face shone with the results of their morning exertions.

"That lets her off the hook."

"What?"

He laughed. "Nothing. Forget it." He kissed her white shoulder, marvelling at the young woman's beauty. "Are you sure you're okay, I mean with everything that's happened?"

She nodded. "I guess I never really trusted my father, but I had no idea that he was behind all that killing." She shivered and laid her head on his shoulder.

A familiar scent blossomed in his nose. "What's that perfume you're wearing?" He sniffed her hair. "It's been bugging me ever since I wrapped you in my arms. It isn't roses, is it?"

Lacey pushed him onto the mattress and flung her body on top of his. "No," she said, nibbling on his stubbly chin. "Jasmine."